"Open! Open!" she shouted, driving the pedals down hard towards the green swathes of holly and ivy. The windspinner whirred silver and gold on her handlebars, sharp as blades now. She steered the bike towards the green boulders. Tam raced after her, pedalling as fast as he could. He closed his eyes – surely the bikes were going to crash into the boulders – and then opened them again because he could not bear not to look. And silently, the boulders rolled apart. Aunt California cruised through into the green passage.

YOUNG CORGI BOOKS

Young Corgi books are perfect when you are looking for great books to read on your own. They are full of exciting stories and entertaining pictures. There are funny books, scary books, spine-tingling stories and mysterious ones.

Whatever your interests you'll find something in Young Corgi to suit you: from families to football, from animals to ghosts. The books are written by some of the most famous and popular of today's children's authors, and by some of the best new talents, too.

Whether you read one chapter a night, or devour the whole book in one sitting, you'll love Young Corgi books. The more you read, the more you'll want to read!

Other Young Corgi books to get your teeth into

The Starburster by Berlie Doherty
The Humming Machine by Berlie Doherty
Joe v. the Fairies by Emily Smith
Jack Slater, Monster Investigator by John Dougherty
Billy Wizard by Chris Priestley

www.berliedoherty.com

The Windspinner

Berlie Doherty

Illustrated by Lesley Harker

YOUNG CORGI

THE WINDSPINNER
A YOUNG CORGI BOOK 978 0 552 55574 6

Published in Great Britain by Young Corgi,
an imprint of Random House Children's Books
A Random House Group Company

This edition published 2008

1 3 5 7 9 10 8 6 4 2

Set in Bembo MT Schoolbook

Young Corgi Books are published by Random House Children's Books,
61–63 Uxbridge Road, London W5 5SA

www.**kids**at**randomhouse**.co.uk
www.**rbooks**.co.uk

Addresses for companies within The Random House Group Limited
can be found at: www.randomhouse.co.uk/offices.htm

THE RANDOM HOUSE GROUP Limited Reg. No. 954009

A CIP catalogue record for this book is available from the British Library.

Printed and bound in Great Britain by
CPI Bookmarque, Croydon, CR0 4TD

Contents

This is what happened last time:

Oban, the king of the fairies, just loved Great-grandpa Toby's humming machine. It was really a harmonica, and sometimes it sounded wonderful, and sometimes it didn't, but he wanted it because he loved man-magic. He wanted it as much as he had wanted Great-grandpa Toby's starburster, which was really a kaleidoscope. He sent his fairy daughter, Pix, to bring Great-grandpa Toby and Tam to Faery, but she had to turn Great-grandpa into a nine-year-old boy to get him there. He was given a fairy name, Tobit, and was captured by Oban's mother, the fearsome Damson-hag. Tam found him with the help of the oldest fairy of them all, the terrifying Flame-reader. With the Blue Bear and Pix he rescued Tobit and locked the Damson-hag inside her own golden cage. At last they came face to face with King Oban, who made Tobit change places with him, and told Tam that he wanted to go back home with him and learn about man-magic.

The Secret

Tam had a secret. It was such a wonderful, exciting, strange, troublesome secret that he knew he had to share it with someone. All night he kept thinking about it, wondering whether he had dreamed everything that had happened, but as soon as it was daylight he could make out a strange blue light at the end of his bed. When the blue light grew stronger, it was just possible to make out a figure, shimmering so brightly that it hurt Tam's eyes to look at him. He knew it was Oban.

"So you really are here," he sighed. "I thought it was a magic dream."

"Don't tell anyone who I am," Oban

said. "I want to be a secret. Don't tell them anything about my kingdom."

"All right, but you mustn't let anyone see you," Tam said. "I can't pretend you're just an ordinary person, can I?"

They touched hands, and the blue light disappeared, but the air in Tam's room had a strange, fluttering kind of excitement about it, and Tam could tell that Oban was still there.

But he knew it was going to be very hard, keeping such a huge secret from his parents. When he went downstairs for breakfast, he felt as if he was bursting, as if he had *I've got a secret* written all over his forehead, as if you only had to look into his eyes to know what it was. He very nearly told Mum, just before he went to school.

"Everything all right, Tam?" she asked, and he nearly blurted it out then and there, but Tam's little sister Baby Blue fell over and had to be comforted, and then the moment was gone, because Dad started asking if anyone had seen his lunchbox.

"I know I made my sandwiches last night," he said. "Lovely smelly stilton cheese sandwiches. And yours have gone too, Tam. What's going on?"

Tam knew very well what had

happened to the sandwiches. Well, he could answer that bit without letting any secrets out.

"I ate mine, and Great-grandpa Toby ate yours," he said.

"What, in the middle of the night?" Dad asked. "Whatever for?"

"Erm, we were hungry," Tam said. "But it wasn't last night, it was ages ago," and then he shut up, because he remembered that time was different in that other place he had been to. He rooted around in his school bag and brought out the two empty lunchboxes. He couldn't help smiling inside himself to think that they'd been all the way to Faery and back.

"I'll have to make more, but there's no smelly stilton left," Dad grumbled. "And where is Great-grandpa Toby anyway? He's usually blowing that humming machine of his by now, the noisy old nuisance."

"He's out," said Tam.

"*Out?* Where out, at this time of the morning?"

Tam ran upstairs, feeling miserable. There was no way he could tell Mum and Dad where Great-grandpa Toby really was. They'd never believe him, and it was all part of the terrible, wonderful secret. They would probably never see him again either. How could he tell them that?

He could hear Mum running up the stairs to look in Great-grandpa's room. "His bed's not been slept in!" she shouted down the stairs. "He's been out all night!"

Tam flung himself on his bed. Spinner,

his little silver
spider who
had come
home
with him
from
Faery,
danced up to him across the pillow,
singing a sweet, comforting song. "Ssh!"
said Tam. "Don't let them hear you!"

Spinner curled up into a ball and
bobbed back up the lampshade, tucking
her silvery thread behind her as she did so.
Baby Blue crawled into the room, tugging
her favourite teddy along
with her. She propped
herself up into a
wobbly sitting
position and
pressed Teddy's
tummy.

"My word!"

Teddy growled, sounding just like Great-grandpa.

Mum rushed to the room. "Here he is," she called to Dad, and then stopped, staring around. "That's funny, I was sure I heard his voice then," she said.

Tam picked up Teddy in case Blue pressed his tummy again.

"No Great-grandpa here," he said. "Keep quiet," he whispered to the bear. When the fairy Pix had turned Great-grandpa Toby into a nine-year-old boy, she had left his voice behind in Blue's teddy bear, in case he ever needed it again. How could Tam tell Mum that all that was left of Great-grandpa Toby was his growly old voice? He didn't know where to start, so he didn't begin at all. He just frowned at Teddy and put him carefully on the shelf, well out of Blue's way.

"Get yourself ready for school," Mum

told Tam. She propped Blue up in the little baby chair that was kept in Tam's room so that they could listen to bedtime stories together. "I'll bath you in a minute, Baby Blue. I'm going to ring Great-aunt California to see if she's heard anything from him."

Blue chuckled up at Tam. Tam wondered if it counted, telling secrets to a baby who wouldn't understand, and who couldn't talk yet. She certainly wouldn't be able to pass the secret on. He decided to try. He had to tell somebody.

"Blue," he said. "Guess where Great-grandpa Toby is?"

As soon as he said that, the air around him shivered with hundreds of tiny blue sparks.

"You promised. You promised!" a voice thundered. Blue burped in fright as the strangest person she had ever seen appeared: a tall creature with wild silver

hair like the fluff on a dandelion, and eyes
like round golden suns. He was dressed in
a cloak that shifted and shimmered

from white to silver to blue and back
again.

"And you promised to keep hidden!"
hissed Tam. "Disappear, Oban!"

For a second the two glared at each

other, Tam and the glimmering stranger, and then Mum called up the stairs, "School, Tam!"

The stranger disappeared; Tam ran downstairs. Blue clapped her hands together, not knowing whether to laugh with wonder or cry with fright.

"My word," Teddy growled, all on his own on his shelf.

Back to School

It was bewildering for Tam to be back in the swirl of the schoolyard again. Apparently he had only been away from home for one night. No one had missed him, and yet so much had happened that he seemed to have been away for ages; weeks and weeks. He had had so many wonderful adventures and survived so many dangers, and all because of Great-grandpa Toby's humming machine. None of his school friends had ever been through anything like that, he was quite sure, and yet he had no way of sharing it with them. It was all part of the incredible secret. If only he could tell Shaz or Harry.

"What did you do last night?" he asked Harry.

"Watched telly, went to bed," Harry said.

"What did you do?" he asked Shaz.

Shaz shrugged. "Played a computer game with my dad."

Tam glanced round. "Ask me what I did," he whispered.

"All right. What did you do?" Shaz asked.

"I can't tell you! But it was really exciting," Tam yelled. He ran away and the boys started chasing him, but they were suddenly distracted by something that was happening by the school gate and they ran off in the other direction. One of the girls, Molly, was shouting to her friends, giggling about something that she had just seen. At that moment they were all called in for the end of break, and once again Tam had lost the chance of giving anyone a clue about his secret.

"What was all that about, Molly?" Mrs Ryan asked. "I could hear you shouting about something in the playground."

Full of excitement and importance, Molly told her that she had just seen a strange person peering through the railings.

"He was really weird," Molly giggled. "Really, really weird."

"A stranger?" Mrs Ryan said, frowning. "What was he like?"

"He had fluffy silver hair, and he was dressed in funny shiny clothes," Molly said. "He was a bit like a boy but he wasn't a boy really. Perhaps he was an angel."

Tam's heart started thumping. He knew exactly who it was. So Oban had followed him to school. Right, he thought, if Oban could break his promise, so could he. But everyone was laughing at Molly.

They all thought she was just making it up. If they didn't believe her, they were hardly likely to believe Tam if he said, "Oh, don't worry about him, he's just the king of the fairies." So he kept his head down and his mouth shut. He willed Oban to go back home and hide in his cupboard again.

Tam slid his hand into his pocket. Something tickled his fingers. He drew Spinner out, cupping his hand round her, then let her scamper across the table for a second or two before he scooped her up and put her back in his pocket again. He saw Molly watching him.

"Ask me why I've got a spider in my pocket," he whispered.

"I don't want to know," Molly whispered back. "I hate spiders."

But at last Tam found a way to tell someone his secret. The children had all finished the work they were doing on ancient monuments. Mrs Ryan said she was so pleased with them that they could spend the rest of the morning writing stories, while she sorted through a big parcel of books that had just arrived for the library.

The children took out their writing books and pencils. Tam gazed around him. He wasn't very good at writing stories. He tried to catch Shaz's eye but Shaz was already scribbling away, no doubt writing one of his usual fantasies about playing football for England even though he was only nine years old. Molly was staring dreamily into space. Harry was drawing a picture of a dragon. And then suddenly Tam knew what he could write about. He could write the most amazing story he had ever written, and it would all be true, every word of it. But he wouldn't be breaking his promise, would he? Surely words on a page didn't count as telling anyone. Mrs Ryan would be the only one to see it, and she would think it was just a made-up story.

Now it was his turn to scribble as fast as he could. His pencil scurried across the pages as if it had a life of its own. Every so often he was stuck for a word, and he gazed into space just as Molly had been doing. It was as if somewhere out there, in the sky outside the window, or on the wall, there was exactly the word he was looking for. The bell rang for lunch, the children tidied their books away on the shelves, and still Tam was writing.

"Finish!" Molly whispered to him, and

he ignored her – in fact, he didn't even hear her.

"I'm sorry to break into your writing spell" – Mrs Ryan smiled – "but it's time for lunch." She gently took his writing book away from him. "You're obviously inspired, Tam."

"But," said Tam, "I haven't brought him home yet!"

"Off you go," Mrs Ryan said. "I'm looking forward to reading this."

Tam followed Shaz and Harry out of the classroom. He felt a huge sense of relief. At last, at last, his secret was out.

The Secret Is Out

It wasn't until the very end of the school day that things started to go wrong again. Everybody was very busy designing the Christmas cards they would be making next week while Mrs Ryan was marking their work. At the end of the afternoon she looked up.

"Children, you've all been working really well. Would you like to hear a wonderful story to end your busy day? Put your things away and I'll read you something really, really good."

They didn't need to be told twice. If there was one thing all the children enjoyed, it was story time. They cleared their things away quickly and shuffled their chairs round to the story corner. Mrs Ryan wasn't holding a library book with a colourful cover; she was holding a pale blue writing book like the ones they all used in class.

"Are you ready?" she asked. They all nodded, sitting as still and silent as they could. They were as quiet as mice. Mrs Ryan would never begin a story until everyone was ready to listen. Stories are so special, she said, that she never wanted anyone to miss a single word.

"It's called, 'The Night the Moon Went Blue'," she said.

Tam gasped. It was *his* story! He bent down so no one would see his face. My story! he thought. Mrs Ryan thinks *my* story is wonderful. He felt a warm glow inside, a glow of pride and pleasure and embarrassment.

"*Last night the moon was blue,*" Mrs Ryan read. "*My great-grandpa told me that anything can happen when the moon is blue, and he was right. Guess what? A fairy called Pix came to our house, and something magic happened. She turned my great-grandpa into a boy who was only nine years old, and magicked him off to fairy land."*

Everybody laughed.

"This is going to be a good story," Molly whispered to Tam. He nodded, his face hidden in his hands.

Mrs Ryan carried on reading. *"Then Pix tried a few spells that went wrong. She turned me into a great-grandpa! I had whiskers on my chin and my voice was deep and growly."*

Molly nearly fell off her chair, she was laughing so hard.

"But she was only a beginner fairy — she hadn't been doing spells for very long.

So she tried again. She managed to turn me back into a boy, but then she turned my baby sister into a great-grandpa!"

The children were all laughing so
much that Mrs Ryan could hardly carry

on. Tam lifted his hands away from his face and giggled happily.

"Shush, everybody, this is where it gets really exciting. Shall I carry on?" Mrs Ryan asked. Everyone settled down again to listen.

"*Then,*" she read, "*the wonderful thing happened. I was flying, really flying, through the blue stars and over the blue moon. I landed in Faery, the place where all the fairies and elves live. I had to find my great-grandpa. I had to rescue him and bring him home. But first I had to meet the terrifying Flame-reader. He is the oldest fairy of them all, and he is bent and twisted like a tree, with gnarly hands and knobbly fingers. He made me chop off his hands as if they were twigs, and throw them in the fire. They turned into pictures that told him where my great-grandpa was. He had been stolen by the Damson-hag. Sometimes she is like a beautiful girl, and sometimes she is so old and bent that her chin nearly touches the ground. She had trapped my great-grandpa inside a golden cage, and she danced to the music he played her on his humming machine. She is very wicked, and very dangerous. She is the mother of Oban, the king of the fairies."*

You could have heard a mouse breathe, it was so quiet in the classroom then. Everyone was listening with every bit of themselves. But at the sound of those words, "the king of the fairies", everything changed.

The air was suddenly alive with blue zigzags, as if the classroom was full of lightning. The window behind Mrs Ryan shattered into hundreds of pieces, drifting round her like coloured stars. And on the windowsill stood a figure with silver hair like dandelion fluff, and golden eyes, and a swirling cloak that shifted from white to grey to silver to blue and back again.

"You promised!" Oban shouted. "You promised not to tell."

The House Is Pixillated

Nobody said anything at all about the broken window. Stranger still, nobody said anything about Oban. As if a spell had been cast over them, the children just stared at the spot where he was standing, and nobody said anything, nobody moved. Then Oban disappeared as if he had never been. The bell went, and Mrs Ryan brushed the coloured stars off her clothes as if she was just waking up from a dream. She sent the children to the cloakroom to fetch their coats, and then they all ran out into the yard to meet their parents. Mum was waiting for Tam, with Blue fast asleep in her pushchair. Tam rushed up to tell her that it really wasn't his fault, but Mum was in a hurry. There

was no time to show her the
broken window in the classroom.
She wasn't in the mood for
listening anyway.

"I've had such
an awful day," she
said. "For a start,
Great-grandpa
Toby is still
missing. I've been
ringing round all
his friends and no one's seen
him. And I've spent the rest of the day
looking for things, and they've all turned
up in the wrong places. The washing-up
liquid was in the fridge, the milk was in

the bathroom, my shoes were in
the waste-paper basket, and
Blue's hat was on a grapefruit
in the fruit bowl. The house is
pixillated! You know what it
reminds me of, don't you?"

Pixillated. Well, Tam had heard that word before. It was when Pix had lived with them instead of Blue, and she had done really naughty things like making the cupboards empty themselves just by looking at them, and the cuckoo clock shout "*cuckoo*" till it drove everybody crazy and Dad had shoved it in the bin.

"I had a good look at Blue to make sure that she hadn't been swapped for that horrible goblinny thing again," Mum went on. "But she's still my beautiful Blue, and you're still my lovely Tam, so nothing like that has happened, thank goodness. But something's going on. Look!"

They had arrived at the house, and could see even before they opened the door that the hall light was being switched on, off, on, off. The television blared out at just about the loudest it could possibly go. Blue woke up, screaming. Mum hurried to switch the television off. Now they could hear Great-grandpa's humming machine being played, very badly.

"So it's him! Great-grandpa Toby's back from wherever he's been, and playing silly tricks!" Mum said. She ran upstairs to Great-grandpa's room, but it was empty. Now the buzzy, jangly, tinny noise was coming from the bathroom, now the toilet, now the kitchen, now up and down the stairs. But wherever they looked, there was no sign of Great-grandpa Toby. There was no sign of anyone.

"You see what I mean?" Mum said. "The house is pixillated!"

She lifted Blue out of her pram, shushing her and cuddling her to calm her down. Tam went quietly up to his room and sat on his bed.

The house was silent now. He knew exactly what was causing all this noise and upset. He knew why, too. And he also knew that it couldn't go on any longer. He and Oban hadn't really discussed what was going to happen when Oban came home from Faery with Tam. All they had done was make a promise to each other: "I promise to keep it a secret, if you promise to stay hidden."

It had been so easy to say, but so hard to do. And it wasn't all Tam's fault either. If only Oban would stop playing tricks, things would be a lot better. He sensed that somewhere in his room Oban was watching him. It was time for them to have a proper talk.

"I know you're there," Tam said.

Nothing.

"There was no need to break the window."

Nothing.

"You just can't turn up at my school like that, all flashy and sparkly."

Still nothing.

Tam sighed. "It's no use sulking, Oban. It's not going to work. I can't hide you for ever. If you really don't want people to know who you are, you'll have to use your magic to make yourself look just like everybody else. Try to be a normal nine-year-old boy. Surely you can manage that."

Still no word from Oban.

Tam sighed and lay on his bed, staring up at the ceiling. Spinner had hoisted herself up there again and was busily making herself a web in the corner. He liked having Spinner here. He'd always wanted a pet spider. As long as she didn't sing too loudly or shimmer too much, nobody else would notice her really. She would always be his now, to remind him of that amazing adventure he'd had. Mostly things were all right again. His starburster was back in Great-grandpa's yellow sock, safe and sound, and he would never part with it again. He had the humming machine, if Oban had put it back in its box.

But he didn't have Great-grandpa, because Oban had swapped places with him. He hoped Great-grandpa Toby was enjoying being Tobit, king of the fairies. He hoped it really was a dream come true for him. He tried to remember how his great-grandpa had looked when Oban had crowned him King Tobit, sitting proud and excited on the fairy king's horse. Was it really what he had wanted all his life? What would he be doing now? he wondered. He closed his eyes, imagining King Tobit swinging backwards and forwards in a hammock made of daisy chains. Backwards and forwards, backwards and forwards, always a child, always a nine-year-old boy. Was that what he really wanted?

Tam must have fallen asleep, because the next thing he was aware of was Dad whistling in the bathroom. He hadn't even heard him driving the car into the garage or running up the stairs to take his work clothes off. Next thing, Mum called up the stairs to tell Tam that tea was ready.

And when he went down to the

kitchen, the most surprising thing of all
the surprises that day was waiting for him.
Mum was putting food onto four plates.
Dad was sitting at the table already. Blue
was sitting next to him in her high chair,
chuckling. And a strange boy was pulling
faces at her.

"Sit down next to your friend," Mum
told Tam.

"My friend?"

The boy who was pulling faces at Blue
turned to look at Tam. At first Tam
thought he had never seen him before. He

was dressed in a pale grey sweatshirt and blue tracksuit trousers. His eyes were a light amber colour, not quite yellow, not quite brown. His hair was pale and very curly. He nearly looked like a normal nine-year-old boy, but not quite. There was something almost ghostly about the sheen of his skin. And when he smiled at Tam, a special, proud, secret smile, Tam knew for certain that it was no ordinary boy.

It was Oban, the one-time king of the fairies.

Spellbound

While they were eating, Mum chatted to Oban as if she had known him for years. Dad smiled at him and kept telling him to "Eat up, there's a good lad," and Blue chuckled and gurgled sweetly every time he looked at her.

He's charmed them, Tam thought. Enchanted them, just like the Damson-hag enchanted me. They think he's absolutely wonderful. They don't even want to know who he is, or anything about him, thank goodness. It must be his magic.

"Tam, you were right to invite Oban to stay here." Mum smiled. "He's such a lovely boy! But really, you should have told me. I'd have made a cake!"

"He doesn't like cake," Tam said. "He only eats flowers."

"Flowers! He seems to be doing pretty well with his mashed potatoes then!" Dad said. "Eat up, there's a good lad."

And it was true. Oban was tucking into mortal food as if that was what he ate every day of his life.

"Oban was telling me," Mum said, piling the fairy king's plate with carrots, "that his father lives ever such a long way away and his poor mother's in prison!" She helped Oban to some more gravy. "Poor child! And he has nowhere to live!"

"I know," said Tam. How could he say, *Well, he lives in a place called Faery, usually?* He had never even heard him mention his father before. Who could that be? he wondered. The father of the king of the fairies. That must be someone really powerful. Anyway, whoever he was, if he lived in Faery, he was just about as far away as anyone could be. Unless they happened to be a fairy or a nine-year-old boy and could get there by flying or just walking through a green passage that no one else could even see. And as for Oban's mother being in prison, well, that was true, in a way. She was the wicked Damson-hag. She was still tied up with Spinner's thread and locked in the golden cage where Tam and Pix and the Midnight Bear had left her. She had to be. Tam still had the golden key in his pyjama pocket. So it was all true, except that Oban wasn't a child at all. He was a fairy, and he was thousands of years old, but try explaining that to your parents and they'd just tell you to stop being silly and to "get on with your dinner, lad".

"So is it all right for him to stay here?" Tam asked.

"Of course it is!" Mum twirled the gravy spoon round her head, spattering

Dad with drops of gravy. He didn't mind, she didn't mind. They were spellbound; there was no other word for it. "He can stay with us as long as he wants."

It certainly made things easier for Tam, not having to wonder where Oban had flitted off to all the time. Dad brought the camp bed in from the garage and Mum

hoicked the mattress out of the cupboard
under the stairs. They made a bed for
Oban next to Tam's. Bedtime was fun.
They all listened to Blue's bedtime story,
and then, when she was put into her own
room, the two boys had a pillow fight and
giggled for a few hours. Oban told Tam
stories about the most terrifying monsters

in Faery. Tam told Oban stories about
dentist's drills that wouldn't stop drilling
and sharks that lived in the toilet. At last,
at long last, they fell asleep. Tam's final
thought was about school tomorrow.
Oban would be going with him, of course.
Mum would tell Mrs Ryan that he was
Tam's friend and she was looking after
him for a bit. But what on earth would
Mrs Ryan say about the broken window?

In fact, Mrs Ryan said nothing about the
window. She smiled sweetly at Oban and
said of course he could be in Tam's class.
She brought in another chair so they
could sit next to each other, and even
asked Oban if he was warm enough,
sitting near the window. And the window
looked just the same as ever; it must have
been mended during the night. There was
no sign that anything had happened, and
nobody even mentioned it.

"No bits of glass anywhere," Tam said to Molly, who couldn't take her eyes off Oban.

"Bits of glass?" she asked. "What from?"

"The broken window."

"What broken window?" Molly was staring at Oban very strangely. "I've seen him before," she said at last.

"You can't have done," Tam said. "He's not from round here. You must have dreamed about him."

Molly pulled a face. "Don't be daft. As if I'd waste my dreams on boys! Hope you haven't brought that spider in with you today."

"What spider?" Tam asked.

"You know very well. The one you had in your pocket."

"Me? Keep a spider in my pocket? You must have dreamed that as well."

Molly looked puzzled. Oban smiled at her and she dazzled a smile back at him. Oh well, Tam thought, there goes another one. Mum, Dad, Blue, Mrs Ryan and now Molly, all under Oban's enchantment.

Even though she was totally charmed by Oban, Mrs Ryan soon discovered that he hadn't a clue about reading and writing. His handwriting was nothing more than fancy squiggles on paper. His spelling didn't exist. And he had no idea what to do with numbers.

"Oh dear," she said. "Which school did you go to before?"

"No school," said Oban.

"I thought as much. You might have to move down to the reception class, Oban."

"I'll teach him," said Tam.

Mrs Ryan laughed. "That's very sweet, Tam, but it's impossible. He's going to have to start right at the very beginning."

"He's really quick," Tam said. "Can't I just try?"

He thought of how quickly Oban had learned to do things at home, things he had never seen before. Just by watching Mum and Dad in the kitchen he'd learned how to make toast, boil a kettle, set the washing machine going. It was as if these were things he'd been doing all his life.

The funny thing was that at first Oban treated them all as if they were impossible, magical tasks that had to be solved, just like the ones Tam had been set when he was in Faery. *Follow the white path. Look neither over your left shoulder nor over your right shoulder. Never turn back, whatever you may hear. When the ruby cockerel crows, look for the golden feather* . . . Those were the words the Flame-reader had said when he sent Tam off on his journey to seek the Damson-hag, and Tam had been frightened and puzzled, but he had done it. And that was how Oban had been, staring at the toaster as if it was some kind of monster that might jump off the kitchen shelf and gobble him up. But he had worked out how to do it and he had made the breakfast toast, squealing with delight when the toast jumped up out of the toaster's mouth.

"Please?" Oban asked.

"All right," Mrs Ryan sighed. "It's a shame to split you up when you're such good friends. Oban can stay in our class today, and you can teach him how to write his own name. That's a start, anyway. But tomorrow he'll have to go into the reception class with Mrs Hooley. Go and sit in the story corner with him."

Tam began by reciting the letters of the alphabet to Oban, just once. Oban thought for a minute in deep, solemn silence. Then he stood on the table and shouted, "Abcdefghijklmnopqrstuvwxyz," at the top of his voice, and all in one breath. Everybody clapped.

"Goodness," said Mrs Ryan, not even telling him off for standing on the table. "Well done."

"And this is how you write it," Tam said. He wrote the letters on a piece of paper. Oban looked at them once and copied them down on another piece, without even looking at Tam's page again.

Mrs Ryan was watching, her face bright with smiles. "Astonishing," she said.

"My name is Oban," Tam said, and wrote it down.

Oban stared at the paper. "My name is Oban, my name is Oban," he kept repeating, as if they were the most wonderful words in the world. Then he turned the paper over and wrote, *My name is Oban. Your name is Tam*, in beautiful, flowing handwriting, and with not one single mistake.

By this time Molly, Harry and Shaz was leaning across the desk following every movement of his fingers, as if he was a magician at a birthday party, and they were trying to find out how he did his card tricks.

"You knew already," Molly said. "You were pretending."

But Oban gave her such a hurt, angry look that she slid back into her chair, her eyes welling up with tears. "Sorry, Oban. It's just that you're so clever."

"Bet you can't spell my name," said Charlotte.

Without even asking her what it was, Oban wrote it down. Not only had he remembered the name of every child in the class from when Mrs Ryan read out the register, but now that he had learned to spell, he could write them all down.

"I told you he was clever," Tam said. "Shall we move on to numbers now?"

Mrs Ryan nodded and settled the class down. It was time for them to do some work of their own. She let Tam and Oban work together, just occasionally looking over Tam's shoulder to check what was going on, and smiling her approval. It was the best day Tam had ever spent at school.

By the end of the afternoon he had taught Oban everything he knew. Oban could even work the computer, flashing from one program to another, marvelling at the animations and sounds that came from it. "Wonderful man-magic," he kept muttering under his breath.

When they went into the hall for afternoon assembly, Oban watched Mrs Hooley playing a hymn on the piano. As soon as she had finished he slid onto the piano stool and played the same hymn from memory, and then closed his eyes and played something so spiralling and mysterious and wonderful that every child in the room held their breath. And by now, of course, there wasn't a single person in the school who wasn't utterly and completely enchanted by him.

The Wonder Child

It was amazing how soon word got out that there was a wonder child at Tam's school. Children told their parents, parents told their friends, and before long the journalists were at the door, cameras flashing. Mum said they were being a bit of a nuisance, but she was so proud of Oban that she wouldn't have dreamed of sending them away. She bought copies of every newspaper. OBAN, THE CLEVEREST NINE-YEAR-OLD IN THE WORLD, one of the headlines said.

Oban gazed in awe at his photograph in the papers. "How did I get there?" he kept asking. And then he would frown and say, "That's such good magic."

And there was more fame to come. He

was interviewed by the BBC outside school one day. He politely performed his latest trick of calculating how much electricity was being used by the Christmas lights in town, and then he counted the stars in the galaxy by simply staring up at the sky, which was only just beginning to grow dark. Then he raced Tam home to be the first to make toast. They sat on the settee together with Blue between them, feeding her jammy crumbs when Mum wasn't looking.

Later, after tea, Mum switched on the television news. Oban adored television. He thought all the little people lived inside it, and wondered if they ever managed to get out. And to his amazement, there he was on the news, being interviewed outside the school gates.

"It's me!" he shouted. "Me in the magic box!"

"Shush, Oban," Mum laughed. "I want

to hear what you're saying."

"But I'm still out here, I'm here!"
Oban shouted. He ran to the screen and
banged on it. "Get out!" he shouted. "Get
out!"

Mum and Dad were laughing so much
that their armchairs almost collapsed.
Even Blue was laughing, though she had
no idea what was going on. And suddenly
Oban turned round from the television
screen, his face nearly purple with fury.

"*How dare you laugh at me!*" he roared. "*Don't you know who I am?*"

The laughter stopped at once. Tam noticed that Oban's eyes were glowing with a fierce golden light. He seemed to be growing taller and his hair was turning silver. A blue light shimmered around him. Whatever spell he had cast to turn himself into an ordinary nine-year-old boy was wearing off. Without thinking twice, Tam ran and turned off the lights. While Mum and Dad were fumbling about in just the flickering glow of the television screen, Tam grabbed Oban's hand and pulled him out of the door.

"Get upstairs, quick!" he whispered. "You're turning back into a fairy!"

Of course, Mum was upset. Tam told her that Oban had gone to bed early because he wasn't feeling himself, which was sort of true. Dad said it was no wonder he was behaving badly – it wasn't good for any child to have all that attention.

"No more journalists," he warned. "That lad's getting too big for his boots."

"That look he gave me!" Mum shuddered. "I've never known anything like it. He frightened me. His eyes seemed to burn right through me."

"He's a funny lad," Dad agreed. "They're all going on about him being

some sort of genius – how quickly he can
do things. Yet he thinks things like cameras
and televisions and cars are magic."

"He's not quite . . . normal," Mum
decided. "He was chewing a pot plant
before tea. You know, my Christmas
cactus! There's great bites taken out of all
the leaves now."

Tam crept out of the room and up the
stairs. Things were getting serious. Not
only was Oban turning back into a fairy,

but the charm he had cast over Mum and Dad seemed to be wearing off too. They didn't seem to like him any more.

"He's got funny eyes," he heard Dad saying. "I've always thought that. And his skin's a bit blue, isn't it? Shiny blue!"

Tam went into his room. Oban wasn't in his bed, or anywhere in sight. He looked for him in the bathroom and in the cupboard, and then he opened the window and looked out. It was too dark outside to see anything clearly, but he fancied there might be a bit of blue light moving about on the lawn.

"Oban!" he hissed. "Don't eat all the shrubs, will you?"

There was no reply.

Tam closed the window and sat on his bed. He opened the drawer in his bedside table and took out his humming machine, and played a little low, sad tune on it. The fun seemed to have gone out of having

Oban here now. For days he had enjoyed being Oban's friend, watching how he could astonish people with his amazing memory and skills. But what if he was really turning back into a fairy?

Things would be very different if he did. Oban in Faery hadn't been a funny boy who everybody loved. He had been a terrifying king, proud and fierce with the kind of magic that turned horses to stone and fairies into nightmares. He could do anything he chose, anything at all, just by wanting to do it. So far he had only used his magic to appear and disappear, and to charm people like Mum and Dad and Mrs Ryan at school. But what if he wanted to use his real, powerful fairy magic here? Where would it all end?

Tam thought about what the Flame-reader had said to him: *We have no need of man-magic here. We have our own magic. Man-magic could destroy us.*

And what would fairy magic do to mortals?

Or perhaps Oban really was losing his magic, and that was why he couldn't look like a nine-year-old boy any more. What if nobody liked him now? What would he do then? What would happen to him?

Tam put down the humming machine and picked up the starburster that he still kept snug inside Great-grandpa Toby's yellow sock. He hardly ever looked through it these days. It always made him think of Great-grandpa Toby, and he felt sad when he did that. He missed him so much. At least Mum and Dad weren't asking awkward questions about where Great-grandpa Toby was. Every time he was mentioned, Oban seemed to be able to work his enchantment and make them stop worrying.

But Tam sometimes felt afraid. He had made a promise to the Flame-reader and he hadn't kept it. *Find the boy Tobit, and take him home*, the Flame-reader had ordered him. *Will you do that? Never let him come here again. Do you hear me? Do you promise?* And Tam had promised, but he hadn't kept his word. He had left Tobit in Faery.

He looked through the starburster and moved slowly around his room. He could see his bed and his books and posters bursting into tiny coloured fragments, just as they always did, but it didn't really interest him any more. He was too worried to enjoy it. He pointed it up towards Spinner, who was humming dreamily to herself, bobbing up and down on her thread.

"What's gone wrong, Spinner?" he asked.

She looped herself round and round, and as he watched her through the starburster, it was as if she had turned into sparkling fragments of golden wire, and she had lots of mouths all opening and shutting in song. But it wasn't Spinner's sweet singing voice he could hear, it was the voice of Oban.

"I can do anything, anything at all. I can make man-magic, I can break man-magic. I can do anything. I can make nightmares."

Tam must have shouted out in fright,

because the next minute Mum was in his room, hugging him.

"There, there, it's all right," she crooned. "It's all right, Tam, I'm here. You've had a little nightmare, that's all."

"Oban's going to destroy us!" Tam gasped, and Mum laughed.

"Oban's fast asleep – look, in his bed."

And so he was, tucked up with the old teddy that Tam let him borrow. He was smiling to himself as if he was having a lovely dream, and his hair was golden again, and his skin a pale sandy pink without a hint of blue.

"Too much excitement," Dad said, coming into the room. "We'll have no more television interviews, no more newspapers. We'll all settle down and have a lovely Christmas."

Christmas

And it *was* a lovely Christmas. Until Oban discovered the windspinner, that is. Up until then he had been as charming and funny as ever. Mum and Dad forgot about his strange behaviour. In fact, it was as if it had never happened. They were under his spell again, and it seemed he could do nothing wrong.

Oban loved everything about the build-up to Christmas at school. He adored singing the carols. He helped to make the manger in the classroom. He was an angel in the nativity play. He cheered with everyone else when Father Christmas came on the last day of term and gave everyone a book.

Then came the holidays – making

cards, wrapping presents, going shopping in town with Mum. Oban loved every minute of it. He enjoyed making the Christmas cake with Dad and helping to decorate the tree. He looked surprised when Mum produced a clothes peg with a frilly dress made of tissue paper and told him it was a fairy, but he didn't say anything to contradict her. He just smiled to himself and put it right on the top branch, just as Mum had told him. Then, when Mum wasn't looking, he cupped his hands in the air and the clothes-peg fairy flew down and whirled towards Blue. She started crawling backwards in astonishment. The peg fairy twirled prettily around the room then whizzed back up to her branch, a smiling bit of wood and tissue paper again. Tam wasn't quite sure whether it had really happened, but Blue was quite certain about it.

"Again, again," she kept shouting,

holding up her hands to the peg fairy on the tree.

On Christmas Eve Tam and Oban helped Mum to make mince pies. She made the pastry and then let Tam cut it into fluted rounds with the pastry cutter. He managed to cover his nose and his hair, his jumper and the kitchen floor with flour. Oban spooned Dad's home-made mincemeat into each of the pastry cases, licking the spoon whenever Mum wasn't looking. When the pies were cooking, the kitchen was filled with wonderful, sweet smells, and as soon as they were brought out of the oven the boys wanted to eat them. Mum made them wait until they were cool. "They'll burn your mouths!" she warned. "And you can only have one each, mind, and save the rest for tomorrow."

"And don't forget to put a couple on the doorstep for Father Christmas," Dad reminded them. "He's got a lot of work to do tonight; he'll be hungry by the time he gets here. I'll put a glass of sherry out for him too."

"Let me do it, let me!" Oban shouted, dancing about on his toes with excitement.

"Haven't you ever done this before?" Mum asked him.

Oban shook his head.

"Perhaps you don't celebrate Christmas where you come from?" Dad asked him.

"Never mind." Mum smiled. "Let him enjoy it."

"But why is Father Christmas so special?" Oban asked.

"Well, he's not like anyone else," Mum said.

"He's a bit of a magic figure," Dad said.

"He's a bit like the king of the fairies," Mum said, and for a second the kitchen was filled with a silence that was so big it was like a balloon full of air.

"We'll be going to church tomorrow." Mum broke the silence at last. "You'll like that, Oban. And then we'll spend most of the day eating, and you'll like that too. But first" – she held up a pair of laddered tights – "you must hang up your stockings." She cut the tights into two baggy legs, and gave them to the boys. "Blue will have to make do with one of Grandpa Toby's old yellow socks." She wiped her eyes with the back of her hand. "Where is he? That's what I want to know. I wish I knew!"

And then Oban smiled up at her, and she smiled back at him as if all her worries about Great-grandpa Toby had disappeared right out of her head.

"What are these for?" asked Oban, completely mystified. He tried to put the stocking on his leg.

"We hang them on the bedposts for the presents!" Tam laughed. "Father Christmas brings them. Just wait and see!"

Blue was the first to wake up. Her yellow sock was packed with things that rattled and squeaked. Tam had some paints and a torch, a model fire-engine and a bag of marbles which he had to keep away from Blue, a compass and a magnifying glass. He thought they were all wonderful. Oban had some of those things too, but he also had a wand and a wizard's hat and cloak, which puzzled him.

"You can be a wizard!" Mum said.

"Now you can do magic, lad!" Dad said.

"Wear them," Mum said. "My, you look like the real thing."

Oban wanted to please them so much that he waved the wand about and made some magic happen. Just little things at first, like making a cupboard door open and close when he pointed the wand at it or the corner of the rug lift up and down again.

"Invisible string!" Dad grinned. "Well done, lad. I used to do those kinds of tricks myself."

Then Oban got carried away. He swirled the wand at the Christmas tree

and made the little electric lights on it
burn like real candles. He made Blue's
fluffy animals stand up on their own and
dance around her. And he turned the snow
falling outside the window into hundreds
of white butterflies. It all happened so
quickly that it was almost as if it hadn't
happened at all.

"I think I've had too much sherry!" Mum giggled. "I'm seeing things, I am."

Dad took off his reading glasses and rubbed them up and down on the jumper Mum had knitted for him. "That's better," he said, putting them back on. "For a minute I thought I was going la-la!"

"I think you'd better stop being a wizard for a bit," Tam whispered to Oban.

It was all very well doing pretty little tricks like that, but he knew that Oban could do something much more powerful if he felt like showing off. He wouldn't need a wizard's wand from the supermarket to do it either. He could feel a kind of thrill in the air, a kind of trembling around Oban, and it made him afraid.

"You can play with my magnifying glass instead if you like."

"Oh, that's much better," Oban said. He dropped the wand and held the magnifying glass up to Blue, so that when he looked through it, her face loomed towards him like a balloon. "Magic!" he laughed. "Real man-magic! How does it do that?"

After the presents came the meal. Tam and Oban set the table while Mum put the last touches to the vegetables and Dad stirred the gravy. Oban munched some holly to keep him going. He seemed to be able to eat as much mortal food as anyone else as long as he started off with flowers or plants.

"Doesn't that prickle you?" Tam asked.

"It tickled a bit," Oban admitted. "But it tastes delicious. Want some?"

Tam pulled a face and shook his head. "Don't eat the berries. They're poisonous."

"Even to fairies?"

"Shush!"

Mum bustled in with the roast turkey. Dad followed, carrying Blue, and they all sat down to their Christmas meal. Mum started crying straight away.

"I wish we knew what had happened to Grandpa Toby," she said, blowing her nose on her serviette. "I do miss him."

"He's always wandering off somewhere," Dad reminded her. "He cycled round the world when he was seventy-five, remember? It was the year we got married, and he never said a word to anyone about his plans. And only five years ago he went on a bus trip to China without telling anyone. He'll be back when it suits him." He piled turkey onto all the plates. "I think he'd fly to the moon if he had half a chance. And it's much quieter without him. Think of the shindig he used to make with that blessed harmonica. What did he use to call it?"

"His humming machine," Oban said. "I love to hear him play it."

Mum stared at him. "But you've never

even met him, Oban."

There was a queer silence in the room. Tam held his breath. Oban had gone too far this time. Blue looked from one to the other of them and started to sob.

"Tam's told me so much about Great-grandpa Toby, I feel as if I've known him all my life," Oban said. "I can imagine what his humming machine sounded like. I wish he was my great-grandpa too," he sighed. Mum leaned across the table and patted his hand.

"Talking of which," Dad said at last, "we've forgotten all about his Christmas present for Tam! He bought it for you the day before he disappeared, Tam. It's been in the shed for so long that it went clean out of my head."

"A present from Great-grandpa Toby!" Tam shouted. "Can I get it now?"

"No!" Mum and Dad both shouted at once.

"I've slaved in the kitchen all morning," Mum said.

"I've peeled all those sprouts," Dad said.

"So eat your dinner first," they both said.

It wasn't too hard, eating Christmas dinner. But as soon as the mince pies and brandy sauce were finished, and Mum and Dad and Blue all dropped off to sleep in front of the fire, Tam and Oban rushed outside into the back garden. It had stopped snowing. The sky was glassy blue and the air felt as sharp as needles. They ran to the shed, tussling to be the first to go in. There it was, leaning in the corner with a piece of shiny red Christmas foil draped over it. Tam pulled away the paper and gasped with delight.

"A new bike!" he breathed. "A really and truly brand-new bike! Oh, Great-grandpa Toby! If only he knew how much I wanted one. My old one is miles too

small now and it's gone rusty and the
chain keeps coming off and Mum backed
the car into it," he explained to Oban.
"You can have it if you want. Oh wow!
My new bike!"

He ran his hands lovingly up and
down the shiny frame, pinged his
fingernails against the spokes to make
them trill, and wheeled the bike outside.

There was a silver and gold plastic windmill wired onto the handlebars, and a shiny bell with a picture of Dennis the Menace on it. Dangling from it was a note in Great-grandpa Toby's scrawly handwriting.

Happy Christmas, Tam. I hope you have many wonderful adventures with this windspinner.

The Windspinner from Great-grandpa Toby

"A windspinner!" Tam laughed. "Great-grandpa always has his own name for things." He swung his leg over the bicycle frame and cycled down the path, and back again, and down again. Even though there was snow on the ground, the covering was soft and light enough to ride on without skidding. He wheeled the bike out onto the pavement. There was no one in sight. It was as if all the world had fallen asleep after Christmas dinner.

"Let me ride it!" Oban ran out after him.

"No! It's mine! It's mine! It's all mine!" Tam shouted.

He rode off down the street, with

Oban running after him. They were both screeching with excitement.

"I can go to school on it! I can go down the park, and round the lake, and everywhere in the world on it! I can ride it to America and see Great-great-aunt California!" Tam laughed. "I love it! I love my windspinner! Yee-hah!" he yelled, sticking his legs out. "I'm flying!"

When he came back, Oban was waiting for him exactly where he had left him. "Now it's my turn. My turn! My turn!" he shouted.

"OK, OK," Tam said unwillingly. He wheeled the bike back into the garden. "Just in here. And very slowly, in case you fall off and scratch it."

It was just as well that he thought of that. Oban had no idea how to ride a bike. He couldn't get the hang of it. He couldn't balance, he couldn't make the wheels turn round, he couldn't even sit on it properly. All he could do was wobble, teeter to one side, and fall off. At first he thought it was funny; they both did. Tam was obviously anxious about his bike and kept his arms out ready to catch it as it fell yet again.

But after a bit, Oban started getting angry. If he tried once he tried a hundred times, and never succeeded in turning the pedals without falling off.

"That's enough," Tam said.

Oban picked himself up again and rubbed his elbow. "No. Another go."

"I'm getting cold," Tam said as Oban fell off again.

"Just one more try," Oban insisted.

"Let's go in." Tam caught the bike by its handlebars.

"No! No! *No!*" Oban screamed. "Teach me the magic! Teach me the magic!" He flicked the plastic windmill to make it turn, but it just did one rotation and then stopped.

"It's easy. It's just balance. All of a sudden you'll get it, and you'll never fall off again. But please let me have the bike back, Oban. You'll break it. You can have my old one – you can fall off that as much as you like!"

Tam ran to the garage and wheeled
out his old bike. You could tell by looking
at it that it was too small for Oban, and
anyway, the frame was a bit bent where
Mum had backed the car into it.
Meanwhile, Oban was still falling off the
new one and getting more and more
furious with it.

"*Make the magic work!*" he roared. "I command you!"

Mum came out into the garden then – just in time to see Oban's fierce golden eyes burning into Tam. His skin was shimmering with a strange silver-blue light.

"Oban," she said, with a tremble of fright in her voice. "Stop that at once. And

I want to know who you really are, and where you've really come from."

But Mum didn't find out, because the blue light went out and Oban simply vanished, just as if he had never been.

Vanished

Christmas Day was very quiet after that. Dad washed the dishes, Tam helped to dry them, Blue woke up and played with her toys. Tam had tried to tell Mum the whole story, but she wouldn't believe any of it and told him to stop being silly.

"King of the fairies, indeed! He's got funny ways, that child. We did our best for him, but I've had enough. If he turns up again, I'll hand him over to the authorities, Christmas or no Christmas. He's a very clever little boy but we should never have bought him that wizard's outfit. He's gone too far this time. He frightened the life out of me when he lit up like that and did that vanishing trick. Pff! He probably used some kind of firework to make that blue light. But king of the fairies! No, I don't believe that."

"Mum, if you want to know anything about Oban, you've got to believe in magic. Real magic," Tam said.

And Mum laughed. "There's no such thing. Now, tell me honestly. Where did you meet him?"

So Tam stopped trying to explain about the green passage that led to Faery. He simply said that Oban had followed him home from the park one day. Mum found that easier to believe.

"He's a waif and stray," she said. "Poor little mite. Well, I'm worried about him, I am. No child should be left to wander around on his own like that. If he doesn't turn up soon, I think I'd better tell the police."

Oban's enchantment must be wearing off, Tam thought, worried. Mum had never mentioned telling the police about him before. And if she does tell them, they might ask me all sorts of questions that I can't answer.

When Tam went up to bed that night, he half expected to find Oban tucked up and fast asleep in the bed next to him, as if nothing had happened. But he wasn't there. The room felt very cold and quiet without him. Could Mum be right after all? Was there no such thing as magic? Maybe it was something that only children and Great-grandpa Toby believed in. He knew that only nine-year-olds could go to Faery. Did that mean that when he was ten, all the magic would go, and he'd never believe in it any more? But he was going to be ten next week!

Spinner bobbed down from the ceiling and tucked herself into the palm of Tam's hand.

"Spinner!" Tam laughed. "Of course there's such a thing as magic! I went to

Faery, didn't I?
That's where
I met you!
But what's
happening?
Where's Oban
gone?"

And Spinner
sang in her high,
spirally voice,

"*Away and afar, away and afar,*
Burst the heart of the bluest star."

"I don't understand," said Tam.
She sang again:

"*Away and afar, away and afar,*
Burst the heart of the bluest star."

"Burst a star? Can I do that?" And
then Tam realized what Spinner meant.

"Of course I can!"

He went to his drawer, took out the starburster and ran to the window. The sky was brilliant with stars, like a field of crystal flowers. Now he could see that they weren't all silvery white. Some of them were tinged with colour, glowing blue like sapphires. He knew that colour well. Sapphire stars meant magic. The stars had been sapphire the night Blue was stolen. They had been

sapphire the night
Great-grandpa
Toby changed
into a nine-
year-old boy
and was taken
to Faery. Sapphire
stars meant that the
fairies were about.

Tam felt a fizz of excitement. He looked around until he saw one particular star that was brighter and bluer than any of the others in the sky. He lifted up the starburster, trained it towards that star, and peered through it.

Nothing he had ever seen before, here or in Faery, was as brilliant as the colours that he saw through the starburster that night. The blue star flashed and sparkled, blossomed and fountained as he twisted the starburster round. Then, all of a sudden, it seemed to break into a million shards that splintered in a shower of blue sparks. He had burst the heart of the star!

Now he knew that he was looking straight into Faery. The picture he could see wasn't split up into little coloured fragments any more, as it usually was when he looked through the starburster. It was as if he was looking through a window into another world: the world of the fairies. He could see the fields of flowers where the babies were nursed by Tanta, and where the fledglings stumbled and tottered, trying to spread their tiny stubs of wings. He saw the graceful, butterfly dancing of the older children. He could look even closer. Elva was there; laughing, teasing, purple-eyed Elva, and other children that he recognized. He could see Morva and the other little green elves. He saw the dark forest of soldier trees, and swooped as if he was flying over the Flame-reader's cave. He saw the

emerald forest and the glass mountains,
and the secret tower of the fairy king.
Now he could come in closer still. There
was Pix!

"Can you see me, Pix?" he shouted.

But no. Although
she turned her head,
although she
seemed to be
looking right at
him, she didn't
speak or show any
sign that she knew
he was there. She
had never even said
goodbye to him. The last time he'd seen
her was the day Great-grandpa sat on the
king's horse. What a beautiful horse it was,
with its golden mane and its tail crusted
with jewels. How proud Great-grandpa
had been. The new king! "Hail, King
Tobit! King of the fairies!" Pix had
shouted, and had run behind him, yelling
and cheering with the others, with never a
backward look at Tam, her mortal friend.

"Pix, Pix, I miss you," Tam whispered,
but she turned her head away.

Tam moved the starburster round so he could follow where she was going. Now she was in the queen's bower. A little boy lay fast asleep in a hammock. Surely it was the boy-king Tobit. Two sandy-haired children were rocking him gently backwards and forwards, backwards and forwards. It all looked very peaceful, full of sunshine and flowers. Tam twisted the starburster again. Now he could hear as well as see. He could hear someone singing, and recognized the voice of the queen of the fairies. She was sitting on her swinging throne, combing her drifting white hair.

"How beautiful she is," Tam said.

He moved the starburster again and watched Pix creep up to Tobit and shake his shoulder to wake him up. He yawned lazily and turned over in his hammock.

"Shall I go on with the story?" Tam heard Pix say.

"Mmm . . ." Tobit murmured sleepily.

"I was telling you about brave Prince Tamlin, and how he faced the Flame-reader in his cave."

"Oh yes. My word, it's very exciting," Tobit said. "Go on. You'd got to the bit where the Flame-reader said he was going to turn you into a slug." He giggled.

"That's not funny, King Tobit. Don't you understand how frightening he is?"

"Sorry."

"And then he told Prince Tamlin that he would turn him into a tree: 'Your bones will turn to wood, your blood will turn to sap, your toes will root you to the ground.' That's what the Flame-reader told him."

"That's not very nice," Tobit said. "My poor little great-grandson!"

"And then," said Pix, "the wonderful thing happened. The Flame-reader told Tamlin he *could* do all these things, because he was so powerful, but he

wouldn't. Because although Tamlin wasn't
a real fairy prince, he was as brave as
anyone the Flame-reader had ever—"

Pix stopped suddenly. The fairy queen
stopped singing. She held the jewelled
comb clasped tightly in her hand. The two
sandy-haired children stopped swinging
the hammock and stared at one another,
terrified.

"What's happening?" Tobit asked.

There was a loud stamping. Someone was marching heavily up the glass stairs. A figure strode into the hall; a huge, heavy figure with gnarled hands and shivering hair like autumn leaves, and deep, deep black eyes.

"How dare you!" he roared.

And far away, peering through the starburster, Tam recognized the voice at once. It was the voice of the oldest fairy of them all; oldest, wisest, most terrifying and most powerful. It was the Flame-reader.

The Flame-reader

Tobit slid out of the hammock and bowed deeply. Tam could see that his knees were trembling.

"Welcome, oldest fairy of them all!"

The Flame-reader ignored him completely. He snatched the comb out of the queen's hands and crushed it to splinters.

"How dare you let King Oban leave Faery!" he roared.

"It was not in my power to stop him," the queen murmured. She looked so small and frail next to the huge figure of the Flame-reader.

"Don't you know that he doesn't have the power to return?" the Flame-reader demanded. "Already his magic is reduced

to fancy party tricks to make mortals
laugh. He can never come back to us. He
will wander for ever on the other side of
the green passage, neither fairy nor
mortal. He can't die, like mortals can.
Thousands and thousands of years from

now he will still be wandering there, without friends or family, playing with the toys that men make, the baubles and tricks that he calls man-magic. A freak, they will call him. A clever freak. They will love him and hate him, but they will never understand him. He is not one of them, and never will be, though he will live for all time! And soon, soon, he will lose his magic for ever, his real magic, his fairy magic."

"Is there no way of helping him?" Tobit asked. His voice sounded small and scared after the roar of the Flame-reader's. The Flame-reader didn't even turn round to look at him.

Pix slipped out from her hiding place and crept on her hands and knees to Tobit. "Don't ask him questions!" she whispered. "He never answers questions."

Tobit ran to the Flame-reader and stood squarely in front of him. "My lord," he began, "oldest fairy of them all . . ."

The Flame-reader glared down at him. "You have no place here," he roared. "This is not your world. The other mortal boy was told to take you home. He promised!"

"It's my fault," Tobit said bravely. "I wanted to stay here. And King Oban wanted me to swap places with him."

"*Ha!*" The Flame-reader tipped back his head and roared with laughter. "*You!* Change places with the mighty king of the fairies! Look at you! A skinny little mortal boy! I could turn you into a beetle, and squash you under my foot!"

"Please don't!" Tobit's voice was shaking. "I want to help, if I can. I want to help Oban to come back."

"*You* help him? *You?*"

"I could try."

"He can't come back. Even if he wants to, he can't come back," the Flame-reader shouted. "Only one person can call him home again. And that person is his mother."

"The Damson-hag?"

"Yes. The Damson-hag. And where is

she? Locked in a golden cage without a key, her arms and her legs bound with the silk of a spider, and her mouth gagged with silver stitches that can never be broken, not with any spell, not with any magic. The spider who sewed the thread must unsew it, and where is she? How can King Oban's mother call him home? Tell me!"

"I d–don't know . . ." stammered Tobit.

"I can't free her, and you can't free her. Only the spider can do it. I don't have the spider, I don't have the key. I don't have the power. You should never have come here, you and your meddling boy Tamlin. It is not your place. You have only brought harm; great, great harm to Faery!"

And with that, the Flame-reader threw his cloak of rustling leaves round his shoulders, and left the secret bower of the fairy king and queen.

Tam put down the starburster. He was

very afraid; afraid for his great-grandpa,
afraid for Oban. When he picked it up
again, the blue stars had spun away. Black
clouds hung over the moon. The night was
completely dark.

"Oh, Spinner!" he sighed. "What can
we do?"

The Shepherd's Wheel

Boxing Day passed, and there was still no sign of Oban. Somehow all the Christmas lights and baubles lost their sparkle. Even the presents weren't fun any more. Tam rode his new bike up and down, up and down the street where he lived. The little windmill on the handlebars zizzed round, buzz-buzz, faster and faster as he picked up speed. He jingled his Dennis the Menace bell every time he approached anyone. Neighbours stopped and said, "What a lovely bike! I bet you got it for Christmas!"

He should have loved all that, but he didn't. He kept thinking how excited he and Oban had been when they first saw the bike in the shed, with the note from Great-grandpa Toby: *I hope you have many wonderful adventures with this windspinner.* He remembered how desperately Oban had wanted to ride the bike, and how at first he had teased him with it. How funny it was when he let Oban have a go at last and he kept falling off. But now he wished he hadn't made Oban so angry. If Oban hadn't been shouting, Mum wouldn't have come out of the house, and he wouldn't have run away.

More days passed, and still there was no sign of Oban. Tam had thought at first that he had gone straight back to Faery, but now he knew that wasn't possible. There was no way for him to get back there unless the Damson-hag wanted him to. And how could she say what she wanted, or anything at all, when she was all wrapped up in Spinner's thread?

Meanwhile, strange things were beginning to happen; unexplained, mysterious things, all over the country. The newscasters on television were excited about them. The grown-ups puzzled over them. Nobody could understand them. The first thing happened the day after Boxing Day, when the motorways were full of cars taking families back home after their Christmas holidays. For five whole minutes every single car on the road went backwards instead of forwards. People who were interviewed about it afterwards said it was the most frightening experience of their lives.

"Couldn't do anything about it," they said. "Good job it happened to everybody else on the road, or there'd have been collisions all over the place."

The next day, all the phone wires seemed to get tangled up. Mum got a phone call from a lady in Australia who wanted to buy a kangaroo, and when Dad tried to phone his friend to arrange a game of darts, he was answered by someone who thought he was ordering sausages. It was funny at first, but people started getting annoyed and worried, especially when they were trying to phone the emergency services. The lady next door phoned for an ambulance because she'd trodden on a hibernating hedgehog, and got the Chinese takeaway instead. And so it went on. When people switched on their electric lights, they heard "Rudolf the Red-nosed Reindeer" being played, and the light bulbs all flashed red. Tomato ketchup came out of the bathroom taps.

And every time something like that happened, there was the sound of tinkling laughter.

"It's the government's fault," some people said.

"It's global warming that's causing it," others said.

Tam knew very well what was causing it.

Oban was messing about with man-magic.

New Year's Eve came. The air was cold and sharp, the sky was a brilliant blue. The world seemed to have stopped turning, as if there was no breath left, as if it was waiting for some amazing thing to happen. Tam was restless. In two days' time he would have his tenth birthday, but he didn't feel at all excited about it. He didn't know what to do with himself. He asked his mum if he could ride his bike in the park, and she said it was a good idea.

"Get some fresh air, and maybe you'll stop fidgeting," she said. "I'll come with you. Blue can feed the ducks."

Tam decided he would cycle slowly with them and then race round the park on the special cycle path. But when he went to get his bike out of the shed, something was different. The bike was lying on the floor instead of being propped against the shed wall. The little windmill was upside down in a flower pot. He wheeled the bike out and inspected it for scratches. The same thing had happened yesterday, and the day before that. The bike was never quite where he expected it to be. It seemed to have been moving around in the night.

"What's the matter?" Mum called.
"Aren't you coming?"

Tam shrugged and decided to say
nothing about it. He wheeled the bike
down the road behind Mum. Was he
imagining it, or did he hear strange, high
laughter in the air? He kept looking
round, but there was no one to see. And
yet he had the prickly feeling that he was

being followed all the way down past the playing field and the swings, and right down to the duck pond. And then the feeling stopped, as if he was free again. As if something had let him go. It was weird.

Blue loved the ducks. When they lifted themselves up and beat their wings noisily across the pond, she shrieked with excitement and waved her arms up and down. She reminded Tam of Pix when she was learning to fly, flapping her stumpy little wing stubs, desperate to lift herself off the ground and join the flying fairies.

Blue got so excited that she needed a nappy change, so Mum wheeled her off to the ladies' toilets to sort her out. While she was doing that, Tam did his fast circuit round the park. He knew exactly where he wanted to go: to the Shepherd's Wheel, where the river flowed so fast over boulders that it could make an old millwheel spin round. He used to love going there with Great-grandpa Toby.

And that was where he saw Oban. He couldn't believe it. He had given up hope of ever seeing him again, and there he was, sitting with his back to him on one of the rocks in the river. He was unmistakable: his hair glowed with a silver light, and his clothes shimmered with a strange colour that Tam had never seen before. He was close to the millwheel, watching it spin round and send up spirals of spray. He seemed fascinated by it, sometimes lifting up one of his arms and moving it round in a circle. He was copying the way the wheel was turning, in exactly the same way that Blue copied the ducks flapping their wings.

Tam decided to surprise him. Carefully he swung his leg over the bike frame and lowered it down onto the grass. He crept across to the river bank on tiptoe. His footsteps were almost silent on the grass, but suddenly Oban seemed to sense he was there. His whole body stiffened, as if he was listening out with every nerve to what was happening behind him. Then, just as Tam reached the river bank, Oban became as transparent as water. Tam was looking right through him at the boulder and the spinning water-wheel. Oban had disappeared.

Tam swung round quickly, and was just in time to see his bike, his precious bike, being raised up and then moving away at full tilt down the path all on its own. People jumped out of its way and then stared after it in amazement.

Now it was Tam's turn to be angry. "Hey, come back!" he shouted. "Bring my windspinner back!"

The bike wobbled and fell over, luckily onto grass. Tam went sprinting after it, and reached it as Mum and Blue came towards him.

"Tam, are you all right?" Mum called. "Did you fall off?"

"No, I didn't!" he said indignantly. He stared around. No sign of Oban, of course. He decided it was best not to mention him to Mum. It would only upset her. "Some kid pinched my bike, but I chased after him and he fell off it and ran away." It was nearly true.

"Ob boo whiz *whiz*!" Blue shouted, waving her arms again. Tam turned quickly, in time to see what she had seen. There was his plastic windmill floating all on its

126

own, spinning in the wind, just as if an invisible person was running away with it.

Tam pushed the bike home so he could walk alongside Mum and Blue. Blue thought it was great fun to take off her mitts and throw them out of the pushchair, so Tam's job was to scoop them back up, pretend they were flying ducks, and tuck her hands back into them. It was hard work, wobbling the bike along with one hand.

"Stop it, Blue! No more!" he warned, and she giggled and threw her mitts on the ground again.

As they were coming up their street, they could see a large bundle of purple fluff on their doorstep, with a patched suitcase next to it.

"Goodness, what's that?" Mum asked. "Have the bin men dumped something on my step?"

The bundle of purple stood up, and they both said at once, "Great-great-aunt California!"

Now the fun will start again, Tam thought.

Great-great-aunt California

Great-great-aunt California was the next best person to Great-grandpa Toby. His little sister, as he called her, although she was nearly as old as he was. She only came to see Tam's family twice a year, because she had gone to America when she was sixteen years old to be a movie star, and had lived there ever since. Tam loved her nearly as much as he loved Great-grandpa. He jumped on his bike and raced down the road to meet her, jingling his bell wildly.

"Jeepers creepers, I love your bike!" Great-great-aunt California greeted him, flinging her arms round him and nearly knocking him off.

"It's my windspinner from Great-grandpa Toby," Tam said.

"A windspinner? Hmm. Are you sure? I might have a go on it later."

Mum had joined them by now. "California, why didn't you let me know you were coming? I wouldn't have gone out. You must be frozen."

"No, I'm not cold," Great-great-aunt California said. "Bought myself a new coat in the sales in town and I feel as warm as a bear in it. No, not a bit tired either. Only been waiting about an hour – that's no time at all. Just thought I'd pop along to see if there's any news of that dippy big brother of mine. Where's he shamoozled to this time, for cripe's sake? Know something about it, Tam? Jeepers creepers, I bet you do!" she whispered.

She followed Mum into the kitchen and sat holding Blue, cooing and cuddling her and smothering her with noisy kisses, while Mum made her a cup of tea. When

she'd eaten three mince pies and a slice of
Christmas cake, she stood up and winked
at Tam. "Now, young man, I reckon the
time has come for you and me to go up
to your room. You can show me all your
Christmas presents."

But although she clucked and gushed over the magnifying glass and the fire-engine, it wasn't Christmas presents she wanted to talk about really. It was Great-grandpa Toby. Tam kept her off the subject for as long as he could. They even had a great game of marbles on the bedroom floor. She was a really good shot. But at last she stood up, stretched her old bones back into place, and then plonked herself down on the bed so heavily that Teddy took a flying leap off the pillow and landed on the carpet.

"My word!" he growled.

Great-great-aunt California bent down and picked him up, staring at him.

"Jeepers creepers. If this didn't look like a raggedy tattered old teddy bear," she said, "I would think it was my big brother Toby. It isn't, is it?"

"No," said Tam. "It's a teddy bear."

He could feel Spinner wriggling about in his pocket. He put his hand in to keep her there, but she scrimped herself out between his fingers and scrambled up his wrist. Then she scampered up the wall to her corner of the ceiling, singing sweetly to herself,

"Silver and gold, silver and gold,
All is well when the story's told."

Great-great-aunt California leaned her head back, watching as Spinner busily made a web for herself. "My, oh my," she said softly. She looked back to Tam. "If I didn't know better," she said, "I'd say that was a singing spider. It isn't, is it?"

"It is," said Tam.

"Well, jeeps!" Great-great-aunt California whistled. "I've lived till I'm nearly ninety years old, and I've never met

one of those before.
I've seen the Seven
Wonders of the World,
and I've never come
across such a thing. I've
spent nearly all of my grown-up days in
America, and that sure is a wacky old
place, where all kinda 'mazing things
happen. But I've never seen or heard a
singing spider. Tell me, Tam" – she lowered
her voice to a scratchy whisper – "is
something magic going on here?"

"Do you believe in magic, Great-
great-aunt California?" Tam asked.

She roared with laughter and slapped
her thigh. "Believe in magic? You bet I
do!"

So Tam told her the whole story. It took a
long time. He was still talking when the
sky turned silvery dark and a tiny blue
star appeared, just to the left of the moon.

He began by showing Great-great-aunt California the shiny box with green velvet lining. "This is my humming machine," he said, opening up the box and stroking the harmonica.

"My, oh my, it's as good as apple pie!" she said. "Can I have a go?"

Great-great-aunt California was a much better harmonica player than her brother was. She closed her eyes and played some lovely old camp-fire tunes, nice and softly. Spinner bobbed down and swayed backwards and forwards on the end of her thread, singing along to the music.

Then Tam brought out the yellow sock, and showed her the kaleidoscope. She peered through it, whistling with joy and twisting it this way and that to make the colours in the room burst inside it. She ran to the window and swivelled the starburster round to look at the garden and the cold blue sky, the bare branches of the trees, and the starlings settling down for the night.

"Ain't the world a mighty fine place?" she marvelled. She lowered the starburster at last. "Well, I love that humming machine, and I love the starburster. But they ain't magic, Tam."

"Yes they are," Tam said. "They're man-magic." And then he told her about his adventures with the fairies – about Oban, the king of the fairies, who loved man-magic so much that he swapped Blue for a goblinny little fairy-baby called Pix. He told her how the only way Tam could swap them back again was to give King Oban the starburster. And then how Oban turned Great-grandpa Toby into a nine-year-old boy and kidnapped him just so he could get the humming machine. And he told her all the bits in between.

"And then, in the end, King Oban swapped places with Great-grandpa Toby so he could come home with me and play with man-magic for ever," Tam went on. "And now I think he's after my windspinner."

"Wait a minute, wait a minute." Great-great-aunt California waved her plump arms to interrupt Tam. "Let me get this straight. Oban swapped places with Toby?"

"Yes. He's called Tobit, and he's still there, and he's king of the fairies."

"He's *what*?" Great-great-aunt California shrieked. "He's king of the fairies?"

"Don't you believe me?" Tam asked.

"Of course I do! Jeepers creepers!" She wiped her eyes with the back of her hand.

"Ain't that cute! When he was a kid, that was all he ever wanted, and now he's gone and done it! OK. So what else is there to know? What's this gold and silver thing that your spider was on about?"

So Tam told her about wrapping the Damson-hag up in silver thread and locking her in the golden cage. He took the golden key out of his pocket and his great-great-aunt nursed it thoughtfully for a bit, then handed it back to Tam.

"You take good care of that," she warned. "We're going to need it."

Tam beamed at her. *We* was a wonderful word to hear. It meant that he didn't have to worry all on his own any more.

"What are we going to do, Great-great-aunt California?" he asked.

"Well, for a start, I suppose we could drop that mouthful and you could just call me Aunt California. That 'great-great' bit makes me feel about a hundred years old, and, jeepers, I ain't there yet. Say, why don't you let me have a chat with that teddy bear?"

"He doesn't say much," he said, handing Teddy to her.

She pressed Teddy's tummy.

"My word!" he growled.

"Oh boy!" she giggled. "That's so cute! Now, Tam, let's be serious. Did you tell me you've seen my brother in this Faery place, through the starburster? Let me have a look again. I want to know what he's up to, I sure do."

She took the starburster again and swizzled it round. "Nope," she said. "I see your lovely room, Tam, and it's all spangling with colour. But no fairy palace."

Tam went to the window and looked out. The sky was nearly dark now.

"Great-gr— I mean, Aunt California! There's a blue star up there, just by the moon. See it? Look at it through the starburster. It might work."

Aunt California leaned out of the window and swivelled the starburster at the blue star. She gave a start, and then a deep sigh.

"Jeep, jeep, jeep," she murmured, with the starburster pressed to her left eye. "There he is – my brother, but he's a kid again! I don't believe it! What an awesome place he's at! And he's all dolled up in sparkly clothes – hey, but guess what – I can see his stripy red pyjamas underneath! My, oh my! There's pretty kids bobbing round him bringing him food – are they *fairies*? What's he eating? Flowers! Bowls of flower petals! Oops – he just gave an almighty burp, and I'm not surprised! Oh, but Toby, Toby . . .!" She lowered the starburster and turned to Tam. "Do you know what? I think he's crying!"

She handed the starburster to Tam, but the blue star

had faded to pale white again, and although it was bursting with brilliant colours, it wasn't showing Faery any more.

"Do you know what I think?" Aunt California sat down heavily on the bed again. "My brother is scared! We've got to get him home."

The Search for Oban

Tam and his great-great-aunt stared gloomily at each other.

"Show me that windspinner of yours again," she said at last. "But just for the moment, don't tell your folks what you've told me."

"They wouldn't believe me anyway," Tam said. "I tried to tell Mum once. They don't believe in magic."

"Humph," Aunt California said. "That's their problem."

They crept downstairs together. Mum was in the kitchen preparing tea. Dad and Blue were dozing in front of the fire. Tam and Aunt California let themselves out and went round to the shed, and Tam wheeled out his bike.

"Boy, oh boy," Aunt California said. "It sure is a beautiful bike, Tam. But d'you know what? It's not a windspinner."

"Great-grandpa's note said it was," said Tam, but she wasn't listening to him. She swung her leg over the frame and sat on the bike, and pedalled towards the street. "You can run behind," she shouted over her shoulder. "Yee-hah! This is fun! I haven't done this in years, not since Toby and I were kids."

She clicked on the bike lights and wobbled out into the street, which luckily was completely empty, and careered down towards the town centre. Tam grabbed his old bike from the corner of the shed. Propped up against it was his toy sword, and without even thinking why he was doing it, he picked it up quickly and looped the belt round his waist. Then he jumped onto his old bike and pedalled after Aunt California. The bike was really small for him now; he had to pedal with his knees sticking out so they didn't bump against the handlebars.

"Keep up, Tam!" Aunt California shouted again.

"But where are we going?"

"I don't know yet! We're going to find Oban, wherever he is."

As it happened, they didn't have to look far. They were wobbling down the pedestrianized bit of the high street, weaving their way past all the strolling shoppers, when suddenly Tam shouted, "There!"

"Where?" Aunt California gripped the brakes and stopped the bike.

"Where all those people are!" Tam said.

He tumbled off his bike and ran over to an electrical goods shop. A small fascinated crowd had gathered outside it, laughing and pointing at something in the display window. Tam and Aunt California squirmed their way to the front. In the

window were several television sets, all
different sizes. They all showed the same
picture, a snow scene with huskies heaving
sledges. Except for one, the biggest.
Hunched up inside it, smiling and
jabbering away as if he was telling the
weather forecast, was Oban.

"I might have known," whispered Tam. "He loves television, Aunt California. He's always asking how the people get inside it. Even though he saw himself on the BBC News one day, he still couldn't understand how it happened. And now he's done it. He's magicked himself really small!"

"And climbed in through the back," Aunt California muttered. "He's a weird-looking guy, ain't he, with all that fluffy hair? Hey, wait a minute! How about if I go in the shop and *buy* that TV! He'll be trapped in there till we decide what to do with him. That'd be a nice bit of fun!" And she marched into the shop, leaving Tam to hold both the bikes.

It nearly worked. Tam watched from outside as Aunt California pointed to the window and the shop assistant climbed in past the other televisions on display there. He had no idea why everyone outside the shop was so interested in that particular set. He didn't look at the screen, just bent down and picked the set up. But a look of alarm spread across Oban's face. He fell over and looked around anxiously, sliding first to one side, then to the other. The watching crowd outside the window laughed, and more people gathered round to see what was going on. Some complained that the bikes were in the way, but Tam wasn't even thinking of moving yet. Now he could see that Oban was clutching something shiny behind his back. Just as the assistant swung the television out of the window space, a blue spiral swizzled round the screen, and Oban disappeared. Tam hopped up and down on tiptoe, trying to see what was happening. Now he could see the assistant blipping the remote control so the television flashed from channel to channel. There were husky dog scenes, reality shows, quiz games, old films, but no Oban.

Aunt California flicked her hand dismissively and shook her head. "No, I've decided I won't have it," she said, heading out of the shop. "Television's just a load of junk these days."

Tam saw the assistant bend down to pick something off the floor, then call Aunt California back. "Is this yours?" he asked. "Funny, it seemed to drop out of the television set!"

From where he was standing in the doorway, Tam couldn't make out what it was, but he saw Aunt California's face light up with smiles.

"Just what I was looking for!" she said, and tucked whatever it was inside her purple coat.

The crowd ambled away in various directions, full of laughter and wonder about the strange TV show they'd seen, and Tam and Aunt California were left to themselves. She swung back onto the bike as soon as they were in the street again.

"Climb aboard, Tam."

"Perhaps we'd better go back home for tea," Tam sighed. "It's getting pretty dark for fairy hunting."

"Jeepers creepers, this ain't no time for tea!" Aunt California said. "We won't lose him now. Didn't you tell me that he kind of lights up blue in the dark?"

"Yes, he does. Especially when he's angry."

"Oh, he'll be angry now all right." Aunt California drove the pedals down. "Let's move. You got that spider with you?" she asked over her shoulder.

"She always comes with me." Spinner ran down Tam's sleeve and tickled his hand.

"OK. Let me have her, just in case."

Mystified, Tam handed Spinner over to Aunt California.

"My, she's tickly!" his aunt said. "I'll keep her in my pocket, if she don't mind. Have you got that golden key you told me about?"

Tam patted his pocket. "Yep."

"Hand it over, honey."

"What are you going to do with it?"

"Isn't it obvious, Tam? Show me the way to the green passage. I'm going to get the old hag to call her son back home to Faery. I'm going to set her free."

The Green Passage

The green passage was the way to Faery.
It looked like a pile of heaped-up boulders
in a cleft in the hill, almost completely
overgrown with ivy and holly. Nobody
would know that there was a way through
there. But one day, nearly ninety years
ago, Great-grandpa Toby had seen the
king of the fairies coming out, and had
wanted to go through ever since. He
had sent Tam through with Pix to rescue
Blue last Midsummer's Eve. But there was
no way of getting between the boulders
now. Only fairy magic would do it. Great-
grandpa Toby had tried all his life, and the
only way through it was by magic. Tam
had been back there many times since,
and had gazed and gazed at the tangled

holly and scrambled over the boulders, but he had never been able to find a crack that was big enough to crawl through.

When they were near enough, Aunt California switched off her bike light and told Tam to do the same. She put her hand inside her coat and drew out the little silver and gold plastic windmill, and Tam realized then that that was what Oban had been holding behind his back when he was sitting inside the television set. She waved it round and round above her head.

"This," she said, "is the windspinner, Tam."

"The windmill?" Tam asked, puzzled. "But I always thought it was my bike that was the windspinner!"

"No. This is the special thing that your great-grandpa left for you. This is what your fairy friend wants more than anything in the world. Remember how much he loved the starburster? He could see magic things through it, because it made the world look different. Remember how he loved the humming machine? Just a bit of metal, but when he blew through it, he made his breath change into music! And now this little windspinner – swizz it round, and it makes the air move! Watch! Watch!" The more she swung the windmill, the brighter the air around it became, like coloured strands of ribbon. "It's making the wind spin, Tam! It's as magic to King Oban as a fairy wand, and he *wants* it, all for himself. He wants it so badly! I'll show you."

She tucked the windspinner into its holder on the handlebars and rode her bike as fast as she could up and down the path, making a dazzling whirr like dragonfly wings in the winter darkness.

And in no time at all, a blue light glimmered towards them through the trees.

"He's ours!" breathed Aunt California. "We caught him, Tam."

The blue light turned back into Oban. He was taller now. His skin was a shining silvery blue and his eyes gleamed like bright golden stones. He didn't look anything like a mortal child now; he looked terrifying. He stood in front of the boulders with his hands on his hips. And he roared with anger:

"Mine! Mine! Give me back my windspinner!"

Aunt California chuckled. "My, you've got a nasty little temper. Now just stand out of my way, dandelion-head. Me and Tam here are going through that passage."

"We can't," Tam whispered to her. "We have to have something velvet, something sharp and something silver!"

"We got 'em," Aunt California

whispered back. "Or we will have in a minute."

"But you have to be a nine-year-old boy to go to Faery. Great-grandpa Toby told me that."

"Hmm. We'll see about that. Why should boys have all the fun?"

"But it has to be on Midsummer's Day, or once in a blue moon," Tam went on.

"And how about New Year's Eve? Look at my watch, Tam. Close to midnight on New Year's Eve! Ain't this just about the most special day of all, when the old year creeps into the new and everything begins again? Past and present and future all rolled into one millisecond? If that ain't a good enough time for going to that Faery place, I don't know what is."

"But—"

"But nothin'!" She shushed him impatiently and advanced towards Oban.

"Now listen, whiz-kid," she told him.
"This ain't no place for you. Your magic is
all cock-eyed here. Where you come from,
you're great and powerful, you have
infinite magic and power, you can do
anything you want."

Oban puffed himself up, glowing with
pride.

"But here – pouf! You're nothing but a
ball of blue fluff!"

Tam gasped. How could she talk like
that to the magnificent King Oban?

Oban was listening, that was for sure.
He seemed twice as tall, twice as grand,
twice as terrifying now.

"Trouble is," Aunt California went on,
"you've lost it. Your magic don't work no
more. Ain't that so?"

"How dare you!" Oban said, his voice
cold with anger. "Watch." He lifted one
arm, and the grass under his feet burst into
flames. Tongues of fire licked around him,

blazing into the night, as high as his waist, as high as his shoulders, higher than his head, and died away again. He stood where he had stood before, perfectly unharmed, inside a ring of scorched grass.

Tam had never seen anything so powerful and frightening, but Aunt California tutted with scorn. "That old trick! If I've seen it once, I've seen it a dozen times. You'll have to do better than that, Magic Mouse."

"Please stop," Tam whispered. "He might do something awful to us."

"No way," his aunt said. "I haven't enjoyed myself so much in years."

Oban raised both hands up to the sky. A shower of stars rained down all around them, brighter than jewels, quieter than snow, softer than feathers. It was the most beautiful thing Tam had ever seen.

"Hmm. Pretty nice," Aunt California conceded. "And it's worn you out, hasn't it?"

It was true. Oban had slumped to the ground, pale and exhausted. Aunt California marched right up to him and stood over him.

"What kind of a fairy is it who can't even put on a firework display without falling into a faint? I bet you haven't got one trick left, have you?"

"What more do you want?" Oban's voice was weak and quavering. It was obvious then that the king of the fairies was actually afraid of old Aunt California. He reached out his hand, trying to grasp the windspinner, but she snatched it away from him and laughed.

"Oh no you don't, bluebottle! If you are truly a fairy, I challenge you to perform one more trick." She twitched the windspinner this way and that, as if it was a tinselly wand and she was a pantomime fairy. "Turn me into a little girl again. Hmm? About nine years old. Can't do it, can you? Too hard for a stage magician like you."

Oban was dazzled by the windspinner. He held his hands over his eyes and struggled to his feet. Aunt California swizzled the windspinner backwards and forwards. "You are very tired," she said in a low, rich voice. "Soon you will fall into a deep trance. You will be hypnotized. You will do exactly as I tell you. You will perform the task that I have set you."

Oban couldn't take his eyes off the swinging windspinner. His stare became dazed, his eyelids drooped. He was breathing deeply, slowly.

"Now, Oban, mighty king of the fairies. Show us your greatest magic. Turn me into a little girl."

"Nothing is too hard for me," Oban answered. His voice, too, was slow and heavy, the voice of a sleep talker. He placed both hands on California's arms, and instantly she changed from an old lady into a little girl, with golden hair tied into plaits, short white socks and shiny silver shoes. Her huge purple fleece was a neat little velvet coat.

"Quick, Tam!" she shouted. "Climb on!"

She swung onto Tam's bike, and Tam scrambled onto his old one.

"Open! Open!" she shouted, driving the pedals down hard towards the green

swathes of holly and ivy. The windspinner whirred silver and gold on her handlebars, sharp as blades now. She steered the bike towards the green boulders. Tam raced after her, pedalling as fast as he could. He closed his eyes – surely the bikes were going to crash into the boulders – and then opened them again because he couldn't bear not to look. And silently, the boulders rolled apart. Aunt California cruised through into the green passage.

"Wait!" roared Oban, and for a second Tam paused and looked back over his shoulder.

"Stay with me!" Oban pleaded.

Tam turned again, and saw the boulders rolling together. With one last mighty push down on the pedals he squeezed through, just in time.

Behind him, Oban and the world of mortals disappeared from sight.

The Sleeping Soldiers

The guardian of the green passage stood in front of them, barring their way with his arms outstretched. His seaweed hair floated around him like a cloak. The sleeping soldiers were wide awake, clad in armour, swords drawn. They had been asleep for a thousand years, and they had only risen from their slumbers to bid farewell to King Tobit when he left Faery. Now they waited anxiously to defend his kingdom from the invasion of mortals. There were hundreds of them. They filled the long cave from side to side and from end to end. They were dagger-eyed and grim-faced, with thrusting, bristling beards. They put their swords across each other to form a barrier that nobody could cross.

"Jeepers creepers!" Aunt California breathed. "You never told me about these prickly porcupines!" She looked over her shoulder and winked at Tam. "Kind of fun, hmm?"

"Snix snee," the guardian snarled, showing his snaggly green teeth in a menacing grin.

"You know me," Tam said. "I'm Prince Tamlin! Remember! I have Vinand'r at my side!" He tried to draw his plastic sword from his belt, ready to hold it out so the guardian would change it from plastic to glistening steel. But nothing happened.

"I guess we need a little bit of good old-fashioned man-magic." Aunt California held the windspinner above her head. She whirled it around, trying to make its wings spin and whirr. It clicked a couple of times and then stood still. The soldiers advanced, sneering. "Do you know any better tricks, Tam?" she asked.

"Maybe there isn't enough air in the cave," Tam said. "We could try blowing very hard."

"Guess I might pass out if we do that," Aunt California said. "I always faint when I try to blow up balloons!"

Tam felt a sudden light movement on his wrist. Spinner had scrambled out of his pocket and was running across the floor of the cave towards the soldiers. She sprang up and deftly wrapped a thread round the legs of one of the soldiers, then another, and another, skittering frantically between them. She looped her silver thread behind her so, one after another, the soldier knights found that their legs were bound together.

As soon as they realized what was happening, the knights started slashing their swords this way and that, striking themselves free of the web that was being cast around them. As fast as they struck, Spinner bobbed between them, lashing them together again.

"Careful, Spinner!" Tam shouted. "Don't let them chop your legs off!"

The cave was filled with the sound of whistling as the knights beat their swords against Spinner's thread. The air rippled as if a wind was gusting.

"Oh, you clever spider!" Aunt California pushed her bike nearer to the knights, holding the windspinner up high. In the whirlwind caused by the slashing swords, it began to spin, faster, then faster, showering the cave with flashing light. The knights stood still and gazed up at it, completely spellbound.

A great "Whee!" of amazement came

from them, and they lowered their swords. Spinner's threads snapped away from them, and they stepped aside to leave a clear passage. They lifted their swords to form an archway.

"Hail, Princess Califfa!"

"Do you mean me?" Aunt California laughed. "Princess Califfa! Why, I don't remember nine years old being such a load of fun!"

"Hail, Prince Tamlin!"

Aunt California led the way through the archway of swords, nodding from side to side and waving a hand as though she was Queen Elizabeth of England, and they passed right out of the knights' cave and into the brilliant, glorious sapphire light of a fairy day.

"Jeeeeeepers!" Aunt California sighed. "My, oh my, this is so swell! I really am . . . I really and truly am in the land of the fairies." She glanced over her shoulder. "Come on, little spider. I'll give you a lift."

She scooped up the exhausted Spinner, who hummed cheerfully and snuggled herself into her sleeve.

"No tickling! OK, we're off!" Aunt California stuck the windspinner into its holder on the handlebars, and drove her feet down on the pedals. "Now, which way, Tam? Where do I find that old Damson-hag?"

Tam looked around, trying to remember how he had reached the Damson-hag's grotto. Pix and the little elf, Morva, had taken him on a frightening journey through the forest of soldier trees, he remembered, and they had led him to meet the Flame-reader. And *he* had set a series of tasks that had to be completed before Tam could find the Damson-hag. What were they? Something to do with a silver path? Something to do with a feather?

"I can't remember," he said at last. "I wish Morva and Pix were here. They'd know."

"*Wish, wish, a fairy wish*," sang Spinner, and instantly the air seemed to tremble around them and a green elf ran and tumbled round the wheels of the bikes. "Plince Tamlin back! Plinpless Califfa come!" he shouted.

"I guess you're Morva!" Aunt California said. "How did you know we were coming?"

"Waiting all days long," Morva said, somersaulting with

pleasure. "Waiting Plince Tamlin and Plinpless Califfa come."

Wings fluttered around them, and a voice called, "This way! This way! Follow me, but hurry, hurry, hurry." A fairy with purple eyes swooped alongside them.

"Elva!" Tam laughed. "Aunt California, this is the fairy who threw my starburster in the pool! But she's my friend now."

"My, you're beautiful, just like Tam told me," Aunt California said. "I've heard so much about you." She turned her head from side to side as Elva fluttered all around her. "But can't you stop still a minute? I'm getting dizzy, just watching

you."

"No time to lose," Elva said urgently. She

flew in front of them,
waving her arms to urge
them on.

"I'm going as
fast as I can."
Aunt California
pedalled her short legs up and down. The
windspinner whirred like insect wings on
the handlebars. "Is this the way to the
Damson-hag's grotto?"

"No time yet for the Damson-hag.
You've come to save us. I knew you would
come. But hurry."

"But what do you mean, we've come
to save you?" Tam asked, panting along
behind Aunt California. "What from?"

"From the Flame-reader," Elva said.
"You must ask him to spare us."

Tam stopped pedalling. "The Flame-
reader. I never want to see him again,
Aunt California. I told you how
frightening he is."

Aunt California stopped too. "No, we ain't here to see no twiggy monster like him. We're here to free the Damson-hag and tell her she's got to get your king back, so we can take my brother home. That's what we've come for, and that's what we'll do. OK? Take us to the old hag's grotto, and then we'll leave you to sort yourselves out. I ain't getting mixed up with no Flame-reader, no sir."

Morva wailed in despair. He jumped up and clung onto Aunt California's handlebars.

"You must help us," Elva begged, twisting backwards and forwards around Aunt California's head.

"Stop buzzing around and tell us what's going on," Aunt California said.

Elva held out her wings and hovered in front of the two bikes. "The Flame-reader is so angry with us for letting King Oban go away that he's turning us all to ice."

"Jeepers," sighed Aunt California. "That ain't nice, is it, Tam?"

"Already the people of the palace have been frozen," Elva went on. "The queen and her servants are all ice-statues in the garden, with frozen vines and brambles growing over them. There is no way for us to turn them back again. We don't have enough magic. It's our turn next, that's what he told us. Everyone. Maybe even you, now you've come here."

A voice seemed to rise up out of the earth and the air, booming and echoing around them.

> "*Ice, ice, my kingdom will freeze,*
> *all will be ice to its very heart.*
> *All creatures in it,*
> *all birds of the air,*
> *all fishes in the streams,*
> *all flowers and trees,*
> *ice, ice, all will be ice, for ever.*"

Morva and Elva shuddered, clinging to each other.

Aunt California turned to Tam. "I guess we have to find a way of helping these guys," she said.

"I know," he said. "But how can we do it?"

"Speak to the Flame-reader. Please, please, speak to him. Please ask him to spare us," Elva begged. "He will destroy Faery. Princess Califfa, Prince Tamlin, please, please hurry."

The Enchanted Forest

Aunt California twiddled the windspinner
for a bit, thinking hard. Then at last she
said, "OK. We'll speak to the boss first. And
then we'll free the hag. Which way do we
have to go?"

"Emble Fost," Morva whispered.

"That way," said Elva. She pointed
ahead to a forest of huge green trees.

"Fine. Lead on."

But Morva gibbered and shivered with
fright, and Elva covered her face.

"They daren't," Tam said. "They're too
frightened to go on, Aunt California.
And so am I. I just don't want to go in
there."

"Hmm . . ." Aunt California stared at
the gloomy forest. "Ain't too scary, Tam.

Just a bunch of old trees. What's in there, anyway?"

"The forest has grown up around the fairy palace," Elva told them. "You have to go through it to get there. And that's where the Flame-reader is, somewhere in the forest, if you dare approach him. He's a burning tree, so he will never freeze."

"I dare approach him all right," said Aunt California.

"But he might turn us to ice!" Tam said.

"Trust me, Tam. I'll think of something. Come on, let's get to the palace and find out what's going on there."

"But don't stop," Elva warned her. "Don't stop for anything, whatever you may see."

"I want to talk to my brother first, before I do anything else."

Aunt California didn't notice the anxious look that Morva exchanged with Elva.

"Poor Kingie Toble," Morva sighed, and Elva put a finger to her lips.

"The sooner we get this over with, the better." Aunt California spat on both her palms and rubbed them together. "Here we go!" she shouted. "Come on, Tam! Let's show that bunch of twigs what we're made of! *Hoi!*"

And she set off with a fierce battle cry, waving the windspinner over her head. Tam felt his bike being pushed from behind by Morva and pulled from in front by Elva. At last they let go, and he found himself hurtling along behind his great-great-aunt.

"Good job I've got nine-year-old legs instead of eighty-nine-year-old ones," Aunt California puffed. The windspinner sizzled as they cycled. Soon they swung into the emerald forest, into the deep dark gloom that was as black and cold as the bottom of the ocean. Strange, still shapes loomed in the branches; bright eyes stared like coloured glass. Tam paused for a moment and reached up to touch one of the shapes, and realized they were birds, turned to ice. The forest was completely silent. The trunks of the trees, the branches, the twigs, the leaves were as motionless as the stones in a graveyard.

"Everything's made of ice," he whispered. "Everything!"

Aunt California bent down and touched the ground. Blades of grass snapped in her fingers, and the sound echoed like a pistol shot in the silent forest. "Yeah," she breathed. "Spooky, Tam. But we can't stop now. Come on."

On and on they pedalled, and at last they could see the white marble towers of the palace. And there they stopped.

"Now, Tam," said Aunt California. "I'm going right on in. You don't have to come if you don't want to. You can wait out here." She gazed at the flight of marble steps that led up to the palace. "But I'm going in."

"Then I'm coming with you," said Tam.

"That's my boy."

Aunt California and Tam left their bikes at the bottom of the marble steps and climbed bravely up to the door. They walked into the great hall and gazed around. There was no singing now, no laughter or children's voices. A deep silence, like a held breath, hung over the palace. Frozen spider webs dangled over everything like white veils.

"My, this is eerie, this place," Aunt California whispered.

She tiptoed through the queen's chamber and Tam followed; *tap-tap* went their feet, echoing like tiny drums in the silent hall. They went out into the garden. Nothing moved there, no sound, not a breath. All the beautiful beds of flowers were spiked with white ice. Stiff weeds and brambles tumbled over boulders in the grass.

So many boulders, thought Tam. I don't remember seeing so many before. With a start, he realized that they weren't boulders at all. They were statues. He ran from one to the other, breaking away the frozen weeds, lifting up brambles to peer at the white, icy faces.

"I know them," he sobbed. "I know them all. They've all been turned into statues."

Several small figures were humped together, some holding hands and standing on the tips of their toes as if they were skipping. They were children, fairy children, turned to ice as they were dancing. The tall figure with sweeping icicle hair was Queen Tania. The little one with her wings stretched out as if she was trying to lift herself up and fly away was Pix. Tam turned to Aunt California, the tears streaming down his face, but she wasn't looking at him. She was kneeling down in front of the ice-statue of a boy.

"This is Toby," she sighed. "My dear brother Toby, I've come all this way to find you, and you're turned to ice! Can't

you see me?
Can't you
hear me at
all?"

She gazed
into the ice-
statue's blank
eyes. Was she
imagining it,
or did they gleam for a moment, as if they
knew her?

There was a sudden whooshing sound,
and the whole sky lit up with orange, red,
gold and yellow streaks, as if it had been
set on fire.

"*Ice, ice, my kingdom is ice!*"

"It's the Flame-reader," Tam whispered.

"OK." Aunt California stood up. "Then
we'd better go and speak to him."

She turned back just once to look at
her frozen brother, and followed Tam out
of the palace garden.

The Burning Tree

Tam and Aunt California hadn't walked far before they saw a burning tree blazing in the heart of the green forest. It seemed impossible that a tree could burn when everything around it was frozen, but Tam knew that it was caused by great magic. He walked resolutely towards it. As he drew near, he felt the heat from it scorching his face and eyes like a bonfire. The light was blinding, but he stared right into the heart of it. There he saw the face of the Flame-reader.

"I am Prince Tamlin," he said. "Why are you turning everything into ice?"

There was no answer, except for a whoosh of flame. He stepped back. He could feel Spinner tickling his neck.

"Ask no questions," she whispered.

Tam tried again. "Great Flame-reader, please melt the ice. Please turn everything back again."

The Flame-reader laughed, sending huffs of smoke out of his mouth. "You ask me to break the spell, and yet you have stolen my son?" he roared.

"Your son?" Tam turned to look at Aunt California, then back again to the Flame-reader. "I don't know what you mean."

"You took my son with you into the land of mortals, and you left a mortal in his place," the Flame-reader roared. "You have destroyed Faery."

"Your son? Now I know! You are Oban's father!" Tam said.

"I am the father of the king of the fairies."

"So what do you think you're doing, turning yourself into a firework and all

your people into ice-cubes?" Aunt
California demanded.

"Ask no questions," Tam reminded her.

"Piffle!" she shouted. "Just listen to me,
hot-head. Your son left this place of his
own accord, and do you know why?

Oh, you don't answer questions. Well, I'll tell you why he left. Because you wouldn't let him do what he wants to do! He's the king, not you, and yet you stop him playing with all these toys that he loves. Yes, toys. That kaleidoscope, that harmonica, this little plastic windmill here – there's nothing magic about them. You know that very well, don't you? They're toys, and he wanted to play with them. You've spoiled his fun, and no wonder he ran away. He's the king here, not you. What do you mean, *Ice, ice, my kingdom is ice*? It ain't your kingdom in the first place! You've got to let him rule his kingdom the way he wants to. Let him bring his friends here if he wants. That's what I think. It's not Tam who's destroying Faery. It's not Toby, or Oban, or anyone else. It's you, you great sparkler. And it's time you were put out!"

Tam looked at Aunt California in amazement. How could she dare to speak to the Flame-reader like that? And how could she say that the starburster, the humming machine and the windspinner were just toys, when they had made so many magical things happen? He felt like crying. Any minute now the Flame-reader would cast his spell on them, and they would be blocks of ice for ever. Why wouldn't she shut up? With every new thing she said, the Flame-reader huffed and humphed, blazing with rage, gathering his magic together.

Aunt California backed off, waving his smoke away from her face. "Jeepers, I've always hated smokers!" She turned round and winked at Tam. "Time for a little real magic!" she whispered. "What do you say, Spinner?"

Spinner bobbed along the handlebar and jumped off, anchoring her thread so that it stretched and swayed behind her, and then she swung round and round on the end of it, a little silver blob making swift circles in the air.

"*Spin, spin, a mighty wind!*" she sang. "*Twist and spin! Spin and twist! Fan the flames, higher, higher, magic the wind, put out the fire!*"

"Get it?" Aunt California asked Tam. "Can we do it, d'you think? Can we go fast enough?"

"Course we can!" said Tam, suddenly understanding everything. Aunt California was making the Flame-reader angry on purpose. And now it was a battle of his magic against their magic; his fire against their wind. They had to magic a wind that was greater than his fire. "We can do it! Can I take the windspinner, Aunt California?"

"Sure! It's yours, Tam." She tugged it off her own handlebars and stuck it onto Tam's. "Good luck! Away we go! One, two, *threeeeee!*"

They cycled rapidly round and round the Flame-reader's tree. Never in his life had Tam pedalled so fast. His legs ached, and still he drove the pedals down. Round and round the flaming tree they cycled.

"Spin, spin, a mighty wind!" he yelled.

The windspinner gathered speed till it was just a blur of light. Tam tugged it off his handlebars and held it out towards the tree. He was so exhausted, he could feel his bike tilting; he could feel himself falling towards the flames.

"Keep going! Keep going!" Aunt California panted behind him.

Tam summoned up all his strength. His legs were like pistons, pumping up and down.

"Fan the flames, higher, higher, magic the wind, put out the fire!" he shouted.

And at last it happened. There was a great soaring *whooosh!* And the flaming tree was enveloped in a black tornado. It spiralled round the tree, forcing the flames higher and higher. The tree was trapped inside the tornado. The Flame-reader's face disappeared; his voice stopped.

Sparks showered away from the top of the tornado, and wherever they fell, the ice began to melt. Trees moved their branches, flowers opened up, birds began to sing again. Further away, the fairy statues stretched their arms, fluttered their wings, opened their eyes. Tam dropped his bike and ran back to the garden to watch. Pix was one of the first to thaw. She squealed with excitement.

The queen's icicle hair began to drip like a mermaid's. She raised her hand and lifted it away from her face. She opened her eyes and gazed around dreamily. "Where's my king?" she murmured. "Where's Oban?"

"Perhaps her memory's still frozen," Tam said. "She's forgotten all about King Tobit."

"He's not moving!" Aunt California wailed.

It was true. Toby was still an ice-boy, frozen solid, staring ahead of him. The sparks hadn't reached him.

Tam cycled back to the flaming tree. The tornado had almost died down now. It was just a few spiralling wisps, nothing like the spinning fury of a few moments ago.

"More!" Tam shouted desperately. "Just a few sparks more! Please!" He whirled the windspinner round, sending acrid smoke into his mouth and his eyes. He could hardly see, but he kept on waving it madly round and round, and at last the tornado gave a little weak spurt, and a shower of sparks bloomed out like a fountain. Tam caught them in the blades of the windspinner and ran to the far end of the garden, where his frozen great-grandpa was crouching. He held the windspinner over the ice-statue's head and whirled it once more. The sparks fell out;

the ice around Great-grandpa cracked like a hatching egg, and fell in broken pieces to the ground. Toby stood up slowly and then kicked his legs high in the air.

"My word, I can move again!" He did a quick somersault. "Ah! That feels better!"

"Want to go home?" a voice asked.

Toby turned round and stared at the little girl on Tam's new bicycle. He peered at her, scratching his head. "You're not who I think you are, are you?"

"Why, who do you think I am?" asked Aunt California.

"My bossy little sister!"

"Sure am!" She beamed.

And they hugged each other just a little, because nine-year-old boys and nine-year-old sisters don't really like hugging each other much. They grinned as if their faces were going to crack, because they were so pleased to see each other.

"How did you get here?" Toby asked.

"Oh, a bit of this and a bit of that and a lot of magic windspinning."

"Your windspinner's brilliant, Great-grandpa!" Tam said. "I mean, King Tobit!"

"My word, I've had enough of that. I'm ready to go home, if we can get there," Great-grandpa Toby said.

"You know you won't be nine years old any more, when you go home? Or you, Aunt California?" Tam reminded them.

They nodded. "That's fine by us," Aunt California sighed. "We'll be dignified, for a change."

"My word!" chuckled Great-grandpa Toby. "I'm not making any big promises like that!"

"Well, anyway, we ain't going home yet," Aunt California said. "We came here to do something very important, didn't we, Tam, and we've still got to do it. We have to free the Damson-hag so she can call Oban home to Faery. Spinner, you run in front. I guess you'll be able to find her. After all, it was you who wrapped her up. Follow me, boys. If you dare."

The Damson-hag Is Free

Spinner scuttled in front of California, showing her the way to go, darting through trees that were dripping with thawing ice. "*Hurry, hurry,*" she sang.

Ahead of them streaked a red fox. "Follow the stinking fox!" Tam shouted. "I remember him – he led the way for me last time."

The fox turned his head and looked at Tam, and there was a flash of recognition in his eyes. Then he plunged on into the dense green forest. And suddenly he stopped, sniffing the air eagerly.

"Can you hear

something creaking?" Aunt California asked. "Wait a minute."

Now they could all hear it, and as they hurried nearer, they could all see it. A golden cage was hanging from the branches of a tree, and a figure bound up in silver thread was hunched up inside it.

"The Damson-hag," Aunt California said. "We've found her. She looks pretty harmless, all trussed up like a chicken."

And as they approached the cage, the hag looked up and saw them. Her eyes seemed to burn right into Tam with such hatred that he was scared to go any further.

"What will she do to me, Spinner?" he whispered. "She locked Great-grandpa in a cage and wanted to keep him there for ever. She tried to lock me in a cage. She could do anything to us if we let her go."

But however frightened he was, he knew he had to set the Damson-hag free.

It was the only way to bring Oban home, to give the land of Faery its true king again. Tam didn't belong anywhere else but in Faery. He thought of Morva and Elva and Tanta and all the fairies and elves – his friends. He thought about little Pix, dancing about excitedly in the palace garden. They needed to be safe again, with their real king.

Aunt California and Great-grandpa Toby came and stood behind him.

"Are you sure you want to let her go?" Great-grandpa said. "She's a nasty piece of work, my word she is. She enchanted me and locked me in that cage for long enough."

"We have to let her go," Aunt California said. "She's Oban's mother. She's the only one who can help him get back to Faery. Go ahead, Tam."

Tam took a deep breath. "Go on, Spinner," he said. "Undo your magic web."

The little spider darted up to the cage. She worked as quickly as she had ever worked, undoing every stitch she had made. Untwisting, unravelling, unbinding, unthreading. And all the time she worked, the Damson-hag never took her raging purple eyes off Tam. At last every thread had dropped away.

Aunt California stepped forward and took the golden key out of her pocket.

"Do it," Tam urged her.

Trembling, she fitted the key into the lock of the cage, and turned it.

"I release you, mother-queen of the fairies," she said. "And I beg you to call your son home again."

The door swung open, and the Damson-hag uncurled and stepped out. As she did so, her age fell away from her, just as Spinner's threads had done. She was her young self, with deep dark purple eyes and long hair the colour of damsons, which fell around her shoulders and down to her feet in gleaming strands. She moved like a dancer, slim and supple and lithe.

"Jeepers creepers," California said. "You're really, really beautiful."

The Damson-hag smiled at California. There was no more anger in her eyes, no more hatred, no revenge. "Thank you for freeing me. You are welcome here, little girl," she said. "You have made me whole again. You have broken the Flame-reader's spell of ugliness and age, of evil and cruelty. I will be young for ever now, as fairies should be." She turned to Great-grandpa Toby and kissed him. "I'm sorry I locked you in the cage. The music you played on your magic humming machine was so beautiful that I wanted to be able to hear it all the time. When you played, you made me young, you made me dance. For a moment or two I was a fairy girl again. I wanted to keep you here for ever, to make me young again. But you don't belong here. I should never have tried to keep you. I will never be evil again."

"Hmm," said Aunt California. "I don't know whether to believe you or not. I guess this place will be pretty boring if there are no baddies around."

For half a second, a snarl swept across the Damson-hag's face, then disappeared as quickly as a cloud skipping across the sun. She smiled at Aunt California. "Depends how much meddling goes on," she said. "I am, after all, the mother of all fairies."

"That's what we wanted to ask you," said Tam. "Please, please, can you use your magic to bring Oban back home? We can't do it, and he can't do it. And the fairies need a king, and he wants to come home."

"And I want to go home too," said Great-grandpa Toby.

"Easy, easy, easy!" The beautiful mother of all the fairies opened her arms wide and called, "Oban! Oban! Come home."

Home

Oban was sitting on a rock, staring at the boulders that blocked the way to the green passage. Then he noticed a light bobbing through the darkness. He turned his head. Someone carrying a torch was coming towards him. He could hear a voice calling.

"Are you there, lad? Come home!" It was Tam's dad's voice. "Come home, Tam! Come home!"

And he heard another voice, echoing from far, far away.

"Come home, Oban! Come home!"

Round and round the voices echoed.

"Here! Here!" Oban called. "I'm here." He held out his arms, and felt himself being lifted up, rushed through the air, moon high, star high. He laughed out loud. His old magic had come back! He was going home.

As if he had been there all the time, Oban blossomed out of the air in front of the Damson-hag.

"Oh boy!" Aunt California whispered. "That's real magic, that is! And he doesn't look like an overgrown school kid with a spiky mop on his head. He looks – like a king!"

She was right. Oban was tall and magnificent in his white shimmering cloak. He bowed to his mother and kissed her hand, then turned his golden eyes on Aunt California. She curtseyed nervously.

"These are the children who set me free," the Damson-hag said. "Be kind to them, Oban."

"Of course," King Oban said. "They are welcome in my kingdom."

He put both his hands on Tam's shoulders. "This boy taught me how to play," he said. "And this boy" – he turned to Great-grandpa Toby – "this boy helped me to make my dream come true."

Toby scratched his head. "Well, you made my dream come true, your majesty. Tobit, king of the fairies! My word!" he chuckled. "But if you don't mind, I'd like to go home now."

They all walked together to the

palace, the Damson-hag with her arm tucked into Oban's, Aunt California and Great-grandpa Toby giggling together, and Tam and Spinner.

"Will you come with me, Spinner?" Tam asked. "Or will I have to leave you here?"

Spinner jiggled up his leg and hid in his pocket. They were suddenly surrounded by the fairies and elves, cheering and dancing because their true king was home again.

"Hail, King Oban!" they called. Pix tumbled around him in excitement, half flying, half skipping, and the queen stretched out her arms and ran to her husband. "My king! You've come home to me!"

"I'll never leave you again," Oban promised. "I am King Oban, king of the fairies. I will never meddle with man-magic again." He shuddered. "And

I never, ever want to go to the land of
mortals again."

He turned to
Tam. "But Tam was
a very good friend
to me. We had fun, Tam, didn't we?"

Tam nodded.
He didn't like to mention how difficult
Oban had been. But he was right. It had
been fun, especially at school, till
Christmas and the windspinner. That was
when things had started to go wrong.

"Can you still spell?" he asked.

"Of course he can cast spells," said the
Damson-hag. "He's the king of the
fairies."

But Oban knew what Tam meant.
"Abcdefghijklmnopqrstuvwxyz. K-i-n-g
O-b-a-n."

Aunt California cheered and clapped
her hands, and King Oban bowed
proudly.

"But I never learned how to ride a bike," he said sadly. "Some things are just too hard, even for me."

"Jeepers, the bikes!" Aunt California said. "We'd better go fetch them, Toby. Can't leave them behind!" She ran off, calling over her shoulder, "Betcha can't pedal as fast as me!"

"Bet I can!" Toby shouted, running after her.

"Califfa has been a wonderful friend to us," Queen Tania told King Oban. "She and Tamlin saved us from the Flame-reader's spell. We were turned into ice-statues. If they hadn't been so brave, the whole kingdom would have been turned to ice. Tamlin and Califfa broke the spell. They burned away the Flame-reader's wicked magic, and we'll never be cursed by him again."

She pointed to the Flame-reader's tree. The fire had burned itself out completely now; the fury of the tornado had died away. Yet the tree stood untouched. Not a leaf was scorched, not a twig had been burned. Leaning against its trunk was a very old man. His hair and beard were as white as snow, and stretched right to the ground. His eyes were as grey as wood-smoke, his skin was wrinkled and brown. He held out his bony hand to Tam.

"Farewell, Prince Tamlin!" he called. His voice was so weak that Tam could hardly hear it.

"Who are you?" he asked.

"Don't you know me?" The old man laughed sadly. "I'm the oldest fairy of them all."

"The Flame-reader?"

"Oh, I can't do that now. Can't read flames, or make spells, not now. Gone, gone, all my magic. Gone, my spells and my power. Just a tree-man now, looking after the king's forests."

Tam realized that he had asked the old Flame-reader two questions without being roared at. He decided to risk a third. "Can I ask you another question?"

"Oh, ask away, ask away. I like to have a question to answer."

"Long ago, you gave me your little spider, Spinner," Tam said nervously. "I just wondered, if it's all right with you, if she could come home with me?"

The old man stretched out his hand, and Tam fished Spinner out of his pocket and put her into the wrinkled palm.

"Little Spinner," the Flame-reader mumbled, his old face creasing into smiles. "Tam, you should know that it's not possible. Don't you remember what you were told, the first time you came here, when you first crossed the sapphire lake? *Nothing take from Faery. Nor food nor drink take, nor sleep have. Go wisely, go bravely, young prince.* Do you remember that?"

Tam nodded. His throat was starting to
ache; his eyes were blurring with tears. He
knew exactly what the old man was
going to say.

"You have been very wise, and very
brave, young prince. And what have you
learned since that time?"

"I've learned that fairy things belong

to Faery, and mortal things belong to mortals. Man–magic and fairy magic don't mix," said Tam.

"And what did you tell Oban about our magic, when he went with you to your land?"

"I told him that fairy magic is dream magic."

"And so it is, Tam. Spinner will be in your dreams."

The old man limped away, with his spider bobbing from his wrist. Tam rubbed his eyes and turned away, to see Aunt California come screeching up on his bicycle, ringing the bell loudly. Great–grandpa Toby ran behind her, pushing Tam's old bike, with Pix sitting giggling on the saddle.

"California says it's time to go, Tam," Great-grandpa said. "But it looks like you'll have to ride your old bike, I'm afraid . . ."

"I liked him when he was King Tobit,"
Pix whispered to Tam. "Can't he stay?"

"He can't stay here. He doesn't belong
here," Tam explained. "And I've got to
go too." He lifted Pix off his bike and
climbed on.

"Don't go. Don't!" Pix clung to the
handlebars.

"I want to go home," said Tam. "I want to see Mum and Dad and Baby Blue."

"Will you come back?"

Tam shook his head. "No. Never. I don't belong here." He gazed around him, taking in all the beautiful colours of the flowers that were blooming again in the garden. In the Faery twilight they glowed like jewels. He turned back to Pix. "I'll never see you again, Pix. I have to stay in the mortal land now. Soon I'll be ten, and I won't be able to come back here."

Pix sobbed loudly. "But you're my best, best friend. You looked after me when the fairies left me behind in your house. You brought me here. You turned me back from an ice-statue."

"But you have your own magic, Pix," Tam said. "You turned Great-grandpa Toby into a nine-year-old boy. You flew me here, all on your own."

"But that's because I was with you!" Pix sobbed. "I can't do any magic without you!"

"But you will. You have to stand on your own feet." Tam pushed her gently off his handlebars. She tumbled backwards, then fluttered her wings and landed neatly.

"See!" Tam clapped. "You can do it!"

King Oban came over to them and drew Tam to one side. "Brave young Tam," he said. "I will make a promise to you, but no one else must know of it. I will give you a special, secret power. Sometimes, not often, when you look through your starburster, on nights when the stars are as blue as sapphires, you will see Pix, and she will see you. Sometimes, very rarely, when you play your humming machine, she will hear your music and dance to it. And sometimes, for an instant, when you make your windspinner turn, you will hear her voice singing. You must never share this knowledge with anyone else, or you will lose it."

"Thank you," said Tam. He knew how hard it would be not to share such a secret with Great-grandpa Toby, or Aunt California, or Mum, or Dad, or his friends at school. Aunt California rang her bell again. Toby climbed up behind her, tucking his arms round her waist.

"Farewell!" The voices of Queen Tania, King Oban, Pix, the oldest fairy of them all, the mother of all fairies, Morva, Elva and tiny, singing Spinner, all rose around them like a cloud of chiming light.

"Bye!" Aunt California called.

"Bye!" Great-grandpa Toby shouted.

Tam paused for a moment when he reached the entrance to the green passage. He made sure the windspinner was tucked firmly in place on his handlebars, then turned for one last look behind him. "Goodbye, land of the fairies!" he said softly. Then he drove his pedals down towards the dark green gloom of the cave.

A Strange Tale to Tell

"Tam! There you are! What are you doing out here in the dark, eh? I've been looking everywhere for you. Didn't you see my torch, lad? Didn't you hear me calling you? You shouldn't be out on your bike at this time of night!"

The light of the torch dazzled his eyes. Tam put on his brakes and drew up close to Dad. He felt as if he would burst with grinning, he was so pleased to see him.

"Is Blue all right?" he asked.

"Blue? Course she is! She's been in bed a long time since. But your mum will probably have fetched her down by now for her last feed," Dad said. "And you'll never guess what's just happened. When I was walking down the path here looking

for you, I was nearly knocked down by a
bike. Seemed to come from straight
between those big rocks there! And guess
who was riding it? I thought it was two
kids at first, and I was just about to shout
at them. But no, it wasn't kids at all! It
was your great-great-aunt California and
your great-grandpa Toby! He's come
home, Tam. After all this time, he's
come home to us!"

And when Tam and Dad got back to the house, there was Great-great-aunt California on one side of the fire.

"Jeepers creepers," she said. "This is good. I'm just warming my weary old bones."

On the other side of the fire was Great-grandpa Toby. Baby Blue was on his knee, stroking Great-grandpa's prickly chin and gurgling sleepily.

"There you are, Tam! Just in time for toasted teacakes," said Mum. "Get yourselves nice and cosy, you two. Great-grandpa Toby is going to tell us where he's been all this time."

Great-grandpa Toby took a bite of teacake and wiped the butter off his whiskers with the back of his hand. He looked across at Tam and winked.

"My word, we'll be up all night!" he said. "I'll be telling you such a long, long story. And your mum and dad won't believe a word of it. Will they, Tam?"

And, of course, they didn't.